DAUGHTER OF FLAME AND STARLIGHT

BY: JACQUELYN BISHOP

For my best friend, **Kay Wojtala** —
my confidante, my compass, my laughter in every storm.

You have stood beside me through every world I've built,
every spark of imagination, every sleepless night of creation.
Your kindness is a steady flame — the kind that warms instead of
burns.

This story of light and loyalty, of courage and connection,
belongs to you as much as it does to the page.

To Kay — my bestie, my forever ember in the dark.

Table of Contents

PROLOGUE.. 6

THE LORE OF THE EMBERWING.................................... 7

CHAPTER ONE:
The Fall of Riven 9

CHAPTER TWO:
The Dragon's Mercy 13

CHAPTER THREE:
The Sky of Two Flames... 19

CHAPTER FOUR:
Fire in the Storm 27

CHAPTER FIVE:
The Cavern of Echoes... 31

CHAPTER SIX:
The Lesson of Flame... 41

CHAPTER SEVEN:
The Shattered Gates of Elderglen 50

CHAPTER EIGHT:
The Shadowborn Strike.. 57

CHAPTER NINE:
Riven confronts the Frostlght Queen 63

CHAPTER TEN:
Riven's First Full Battle With the Flame 66

CHAPTER ELEVEN:
The Sovereign Sends His Champion 70

CHAPTER TWELVE:
Dravaryn Arrives and delivers the Sovereign's first strike 76

CHAPTER THIRTEEN:
Riven Nearly Burns Himself Out to Save Her............... 83

CHAPTER FOURTEEN:
Auren Tries to Save Them Both 88

CHAPTER FIFTEEN:
Riven's Transformation into the True Firebound 93

CHAPTER SIXTEEN:
The true battle begins — and the Shadow Realm trembles 99

CHAPTER SEVENTEEN:
Auren's Final Stand 103

CHAPTER EIGHTEEN:
The Dawn After Shadow 111

CHAPTER NINTEEN:
Auren 118

EPILOGUE 120

PROPHECY OF THE FIREBOUND 121

THE BARD'S FINAL SONG — "THE FIREBOUND PROMISE" 123

PROLOGUE

Long before mortals learned the names of stars, the world was shared by four ancient races:
the Dragons, keepers of flame and memory;

the Fair Folk, guardians of the Veil between realms;

 the Shapeshifters, born of both, yet belonging to neither.

and **the Shadowborn,** creatures of hunger and memory, desperate to return to the light they had lost.

When the Veil began to thin and shadows slipped through from the Void, their fragile peace shattered.

THE LORE OF THE EMBERWING

From the Codex Dracorum, Third Age

"In the beginning, the heavens were flame, and the flame was song. From that song came wings, and from those wings, the world was born."

Among dragons, the name Emberwing is whispered with both reverence and fear. It is not merely a name but a lineage — a covenant of fire older than the stars themselves.

When the first dragons rose from the molten rivers of creation, one among them burned brighter than all the rest: Vaelrion, the Eternal Flame. His wings carried sparks that fell like comets, igniting new life wherever they touched.

From his light came a brood unlike any other — dragons whose fire pulsed not only with heat, but with memory. These were the Emberwings, keepers of the world's heartfire.

It is said that when an Emberwing takes flight, the wind bends in awe and the stars draw nearer to listen.

In the age of shadow and division, when the Fair Folk sought to seal the realms apart, the Emberwings stood against them. They believed the realms must remain united, for if flame is severed from air, it dies.

But the fairies feared the dragons 'power. They crafted the Veil, a wall of twilight between the worlds, and drove the dragons back to their fiery realm, Drakharis.
During that war, the last known Emberwing vanished — a dragon hatchling whose scales shimmered silver and gold. Her name was lost… until now.

Centuries later, the Seer of Elderglen spoke a vision before the Fairy Court:

"When starlight weds fire and the sky takes wing once more, the lost child of flame shall rise.

Between two worlds she shall walk —
between two hearts she shall burn —
and by her hand, the Veil shall mend or fall."

This prophecy became forbidden. The Fair Folk erased it from their songs, fearing the rise of another Shapeshifter — a being of both flame and light, chaos and balance.

But among the dragons, the prophecy endured. Carved into obsidian stones and guarded by Vaelrion's kin, it became known as The Emberwing Prophecy.

In the present age, few recall the truth. The Fairy Queen, Aislyn, calls Shapeshifters "aberrations." The dragons call them "the bridge."

When Lyra was born — part fairy, part dragon, her wings burning with silver fire — the world trembled.

Old powers stirred. The Veil began to thin.
And the songs of the Emberwing echoed once more through the caverns of Drakharis and the moonlit groves of Elderglen.

Sacred Symbol: The Sigil of the Emberwing:
A spiral of flame encircling a single star — representing fire and starlight united.

It adorns ancient dragon relics and the oldest fairy gates, half-erased but never forgotten.

CHAPTER ONE:
The Fall of Riven

They cast him from the Court of Stars,
His wings undone, his name unmade.
Yet in his heart an ember burned,
The fire no curse could fade.
When flame and shadow meet again,
His song shall break the chain.

From the Songs of the Veil, Volume IX
"Even stars bleed when they fall from grace."

The Queen's court gleamed like a winter dream. Every wall was carved from living crystal, every arch alive with cold light. The air itself hummed with enchantment—spells woven to keep the mortals out, the dragons beneath, and the fairies above all others.

At the far end of the hall sat Queen Aislyn, radiant and terrible upon her throne of ice. The great brazier beside her burned with a pale blue flame, its glow reflected in her eyes.

Before her knelt Riven, wings folded tight, his head bowed. His armor was etched with the runes of the Frostguard—first knight of the Silver Court, sworn to defend the Queen and her dominion over the Veil.

"You summoned me, my Queen," he said, his voice steady despite the chill creeping beneath his skin.

"Rise, my faithful," she said. "I have a task that will shape the ages."

Riven stood, though his breath clouded in the freezing air. Around the throne, courtiers watched in silence—dozens of fairies cloaked in white, their expressions carved from frost.

Aislyn's hand drifted toward the brazier. The flame within twisted, revealing an image: A dragon—enormous, wounded, bound in chains of light.

"The last of the Emberwing line," the Queen said. "Its fire weakens the Veil. It must be extinguished."

Riven's jaw tightened. "That creature is sacred. The dragons were promised sanctuary after the Binding War."

"They were promised silence," she corrected. "And this one has forgotten its vow."

"Then bind it again."

"I have tried." Her voice sharpened, each word edged with ice. "Its fire feeds the breach. Each time it dreams, the Veil trembles.

You will go to the Valley of Ash and end its heartfire."

Riven froze. "End it? You mean kill it."

"Call it what you will. It is a mercy to the world."

The courtiers began to whisper—tiny shards of sound like falling glass. Riven stepped forward, unable to stop himself.

"Majesty… the Veil was not built to last forever. Its strength depends on balance. If you destroy the fire, there will be only frost. No world can live in such cold."

Aislyn rose from her throne. Frost bloomed beneath her bare feet. "You dare instruct me?"

"I dare remind you what I swore to defend—the harmony between light and flame. Not your fear of it."

Her expression hardened. "You speak like a dragon."

"Perhaps they remember what you have forgotten."

The hall fell utterly silent.

Then, in a voice as soft as falling snow, she said, "You would defy me?"

Riven bowed his head. "If obedience demands the death of innocence... yes."

The Queen's eyes filled with cold light. She lifted her hand. "Then I strip you of title and name. Let the frost claim your wings, that you may crawl among the ashes you pity."

Magic lashed the air. Riven cried out as pain tore across his back. Feathers of ice sprouted and shattered; his wings, once radiant with silver light, splintered into shards that fell to the floor. Veilblade — his sword — cracked clean down the middle.

Two guards approached, their faces averted in shame. They took his sword and cast it at the base of the throne. The runes along its blade dimmed. It burned against his skin. He collapsed to his knees, breath ragged. Magic bound him by runes of starlight.

"You disobey my royal command," the Queen's voice carried through the chamber. "You spare a dragon that should be slain. You opened the Veil and let the flame into our world."

"I saved him," Riven said, his voice low but steady. "He is no threat to us. You fear what you did not understand."

A gasp rippled through the gathered courtiers. Even to question the Queen was near-blasphemy.

Aislyn's eyes, cold as cut glass, narrowed.

"Fear keeps the world intact, knight. Fire consumes. You have chosen the flame over your own kin."

He met her gaze — unflinching. "I choose mercy."

The Queen rose. "Then you shall learn what mercy costs."

The court's torches dimmed as the runes ignited, binding Riven in a circle of white fire. His wings flared open in pain, the membranes translucent and perfect — until the Queen lifted her scepter.

"For betrayal of the Crown, I sever you from our grace."

The spell struck like a thunderclap.

Light and agony tore through him. His wings blazed, veins of fire racing across the delicate filigree. The sound of tearing silk filled the hall as the edges blackened and curled. Riven screamed once — raw, wordless — and fell forward, smoke rising from his back.

Riven looked up through a haze of agony. "You have unmade yourself, my Queen," he whispered.

Her expression never wavered. "No. I have preserved us."

Her voice echoed through the hall: "Go, Riven of the Fallen Wing. From this day, you are no knight of mine. You are no longer of the Fair Folk. May the winds cast you where even your shadow fears to tread."

The runes dissolved. The floor beneath him split like glass, revealing endless twilight — the storm between worlds.

He fell.

The moon hung sharp over Elderglen that night, its light breaking through the branches like shards of glass. The air trembled with power — the kind that precedes war. All across the Twilight Court, fairies gathered beneath the crystal spires, wings shimmering in fear and awe.

CHAPTER TWO:
The Dragon's Mercy

Through clouds that shimmered with starlight, through endless wind that carried whispers of the dragon he'd saved. The fire inside him dimmed, replaced by darkness and rain.

Seven days he fell, stripped of name, magic, and home.

On the seventh, he struck earth in the mortal forest — his broken wings folding around him like burnt paper. He should have died there, forgotten by time.

The scar of the Queen's magic still marred his back, but when he looked to the sky, faint motes of light shimmered where his wings had once been — not whole, but alive.

Ash fell like snow.

The valley lay in ruin, lit only by the faint blue glow of the Queen's runes. The air shimmered with frostlight even here, at the edge of her dominion. Riven staggered forward, his breath ragged, his body torn and bloodied from the fall. His wings were gone, the memory of them aching like phantom pain.

He wandered for days through the wastelands until the frost turned to ash and the air grew warm again. There, in the valley he had been sent to destroy, he found the chained dragon—the very creature he had refused to kill.

Before him, the dragon strained against its bonds—great spears of ice driven through its wings, chains of silver fire wrapping its limbs. Each breath it took sent cracks through the earth.

It lifted its head weakly as he approached, golden eyes full of ancient fire "Knight of frost," it rumbled, its voice trembling the stones, "you come to end me."

Riven fell to his knees. "I came because I could not obey."

The dragon's molten eye opened, vast and sorrowful. "Then why do you kneel?"

"Because I have nothing left." He glanced down at his empty hands—scarred, shaking, useless. The Queen had taken everything. His armor, his rank, his blade. He was no longer a knight—just a shadow of one.

But still, the dragon suffered. Still, those chains glowed with her cruel perfection, binding its limbs to the earth, each link humming with the Queen's sigil — ice magic feeding on the creature's heat. The ground around it was a wasteland of glass and ash.

Riven knelt beside the creature, his hands trembling from pain and disbelief. "She called you a threat," he said. "But you're dying."

The dragon's eye opened — gold like molten dawn. "All fire is a threat to frost."

Riven looked down at the manacles, recognizing the runes woven through them. He had helped forge that spell once, years ago. The realization hollowed him. "I forged those runes," he whispered.

"They answer only to her."

"Then make them answer to you," said the dragon. "If you remember who you are."

"If I break these," he said, "she'll hunt me. She'll hunt us both."

"She will," the dragon answered simply. "But she will not catch what can fly."

He hesitated only a heartbeat more. Then he pressed his hands to the bindings. Pain lanced up his arms as the runes burned through his flesh — rejecting him, punishing him for treason. He forced his own light into the spell, unmaking it word by word.

Riven looked down at his palms. Thin lines of frost-scars crossed the skin—marks from his years of service, burned in when he had sworn fealty to the Queen. They had always glowed pale blue, tethered to her magic. Now they were dull.

He pressed his hands together. "If my blade is gone, then I'll be the blade."

He closed his eyes, feeling the memory of steel—the weight, the hum, the perfect stillness before a strike. He breathed into that memory, and for the first time since the exile, he let the fire he'd always feared rise inside him.

The frost-scars flared. Gold light spilled between his fingers.

He gasped. The light grew, spreading up his arms, swirling with crimson and silver until it solidified into something real. The sound of metal rang faintly in the air.

When he opened his eyes, he held a sword—not forged of steel, but of pure flame and memory. Its edge shimmered like a liquid sunrise.

The dragon inhaled sharply, smoke curling from its nostrils. "The fire remembers you."

Riven rose to his feet, the sword burning steady in his grasp. "Then let it remember mercy."

He stepped toward the first chain. Its rune hissed, sensing the fire. Cold wind whipped through the valley, shrieking like the Queen's fury.

Riven raised his hand.

"By frost unbound and flame reclaimed—be undone."

He struck. The blade of light carved through the ice like dawn through shadow. The chain exploded into shards of blue crystal that melted before they touched the ground.

The next rune fought harder, spitting sparks and frostfire. Each swing drained him, but he did not stop. He moved like a storm contained in flesh—each stroke unmaking what he had once built.

Finally, only the central chain remained: the one wrapped around the dragon's heart.

"This one will take more than light," the dragon warned.

"Then it can take what's left of me," Riven said.

He drove the sword deep. The valley blazed gold. Heat and cold collided, roaring in his ears. The runes screamed as they died, and Riven felt his strength burn away with them. The final chain shattered. The explosion threw him backward.

Then silence.

The chains were gone.

Riven dropped to his knees, the sword flickering, fading to embers. His hands smoked from the effort. The dragon pulled itself free, shaking the last of the frost from its wings. It turned its head toward him.

"You remembered what you are," it said softly.

Riven looked down at his hands. The sword was gone, but a faint golden glow pulsed in his chest where the blade's light had been.

"I remembered," he murmured, "that a sword doesn't have to kill to break chains."

The creature loomed over him, vast and luminous, smoke pouring from its nostrils. "Why?" it asked.

Riven could barely breathe. "Because no one deserves to die for being what they are."

The dragon studied him for a long time, then lowered its head.

"You gave up your wings for mercy," it said. "Let my fire be your own until you find them again."

The dragon lowered its massive head until one golden eye filled his vision.

"You freed me when no other would. My fire is yours now. You are bound, as I am bound—Fire to fire, life to life."

The dragon gazed at him for a long moment, then lowered its head, pressing its brow against his heart. Warmth rushed through him—gentle, steady, not searing, not cruel but alive. A pulse of warmth surged through Riven's heart. He gasped as his scars lit with faint golden fire—no longer blue frost, but living flame. The bond between fairy and dragon, once forbidden, was born again.

"What are you called?" he asked.

"Auren," said the dragon. "And you, broken one, are Firebrand now."

"Auren," Riven said, giving the name that rose unbidden to his tongue. "Golden one."

Outside, dawn broke in ribbons of color no mortal sky had ever known. The two stood together at the edge of the valley. The sun rose over the ash fields, painting them in hues of rose and gold. Riven's hair caught the light, shimmering faintly with the same fire as the dragon beside him.

He looked down at his empty hand, and for a heartbeat the blade of light flickered there again—an echo of what he had become.

"You were right," he told the dragon softly. "The fire remembered me."

"And now," the dragon said, "it will never forget."

They rose together. Auren's wings caught the newborn sun, scattering flame across the valley. Riven climbed onto the dragon's back, hands pressed against warm scales that thrummed with living thunder.

The first gust nearly threw him—then he leaned forward, and the fire within them synchronized. When Auren beat his wings, Riven's spirit beat with them.

Below, rivers flashed like mirrors; above, clouds parted as though bowing.

He laughed—hoarse, astonished, free. Centuries of exile burned away in that single breath.

"Look well, Queen of Frost," he whispered into the wind. "Your fallen knight flies again."

From that day, rumors spread through the mortal lands of a dark-winged fairy and a golden dragon seen at dusk, flying together.

The peasants called him the Firebound, the fairies the Betrayer Restored, and the dragons Brother of Flame.

Riven called himself nothing at all. He was simply whole again.

CHAPTER THREE:
The Sky of Two Flames

Lyra crouched on the cliff's edge, wind tugging at her silver hair.

Below, the Valley of Ash glowed faintly with the breath of sleeping dragons.

Her mother had once told her that dragons dream of the world's heartbeat — if they ever stopped, the world itself would fall silent.

But Lyra was no ordinary girl.

Beneath her skin burned the fire of a dragon and the magic of the Fair Folk.

She was the last known Shapeshifter, able to take the form of both flame and feather.

To the fairies, she was an abomination.
To the dragons, a lost heir.

And to herself, she was a question no one dared to answer.

She lifted her hand. The air rippled; tiny embers formed and drifted upward, drawn to her like moths. Each spark pulsed once, twice—then flickered out. The dragons 'breathing below grew uneasy, the glow of their hidden scales dimming.

"Easy," she whispered to the valley. "Sleep."

But the world did not listen.

A sound like thunder rippled beneath the earth, followed by a heartbeat that was not the dragons'.

Lyra froze.

From the horizon, the sky cracked open in a seam of light — silver at first, then black, then burning gold.

The Veil trembled.

And in that moment, every dragon in the valley opened its eyes.

The dragons 'eyes burned open one by one across the valley—amber, bronze, and gold, shining like lanterns in the mist.

The ground trembled beneath their shifting bodies. Scales clattered like falling stone. Lyra felt the heat of their unease reach her even from the cliff.

"I didn't mean—" she whispered, but her words vanished into the rising wind.

The seam of light on the horizon widened. It pulsed, deep and rhythmic, as if the sky itself had found a new heartbeat. Then came the sound—a low, hollow cry that carried no direction, a noise that wasn't thunder but memory.

The Veil was stirring.

Lyra's mother's stories flooded back: of the boundary that once sealed light and shadow apart, of the wars that had nearly broken the world when dragons and fairies fought to control it. The Veil had held for centuries, invisible but steady—until now.

If it ever breaks, her mother had said, fire and frost will meet again, and nothing will survive their joining.

The cry came again, closer this time. The dragons below shifted restlessly, exhaling streams of smoke. Lyra's heartbeat matched their rhythm until she couldn't tell where her pulse ended and theirs began.

A flash of pain lanced through her chest. Her skin shimmered; flame flickered across her fingers.

"No," she gasped. "Not now."

20

Her body rippled, the way it always did when her two halves warred. Her vision fractured—part sky, part flame, part feathers and light. Her power wanted out, drawn to the pulse in the air.

She tried to stand, but the ground gave way beneath her feet. The cliff cracked, crumbling into a rain of stone and ash. Lyra fell.

The world blurred. The wind roared past her, stealing her breath. Instinct took hold. Her hands burst into fire, and wings of molten light unfurled from her shoulders—half feather, half flame. She caught herself mid-fall, skimming above the valley floor.

Below, the dragons stirred fully awake. Massive shapes rose from the mist, their wings unfolding like storm clouds. One raised its head toward her—eyes vast and ancient—and she felt the weight of its gaze settle inside her chest.

"Child of both flame and starlight," a voice rumbled in her mind, deep and slow. "Why do you wake us?"

"I didn't!" Lyra cried aloud. "Something's wrong—look!"

The dragon's gaze lifted skyward. The tear in the horizon had widened into a glowing wound, spilling motes of black fire. The air smelled of frost and smoke, and shadows slithered within the light.

"The Veil," the dragon whispered. "It stirs."

Then, for the first time in centuries, the dragons took flight.

Lyra hovered above the valley, staring as dozens of dragons rose into the air, their wings beating thunder through the clouds. The light from the rift reflected across their scales, and for a moment, the sky looked aflame.

Something seared across her shoulder. She cried out, clutching at her skin. A mark burned there, spiraling outward in a pattern of silver and gold. It pulsed in time with the rift's light.

"No, no, no—what are you doing to me?" she gasped.

The voice of the dragon thundered again in her head:

"You have been chosen, Shapeshifter. The fire answers its heir."

"Chosen for what?"

But the answer came not from the dragon, but from the wound in the sky itself.

The air above her split open. A rush of energy tore through her body, flooding her with light. For a heartbeat, she saw shapes inside the rift—vast wings of flame, a figure standing upon them, watching her. A fairy? A man?

Then the vision shattered.

Lyra fell again, tumbling into darkness.

When she opened her eyes, the valley was silent. Smoke coiled above the ground, and the dragons were gone—vanished into the storm that now circled the horizon. Only one remained, far away, silhouetted against the sky.

No, not one. Two.

A dragon, wings blazing gold… and a dark shape riding its back.

Lyra blinked, breath catching. The rider turned as if he could see her across the miles. Even at that distance, she felt the flare of his power, wild and familiar—the same pulse that burned within her chest.

Then the wind shifted, carrying his voice faintly across the chasm, a whisper borne on flame:

"The Emberwing has awakened."

Before she could call out, lightning split the sky between them. The vision broke. The rider and his dragon vanished into the storm.

Lyra stood alone on the ashen plain, the mark on her shoulder still glowing faintly.

"Who are you?" she whispered into the wind. "And what have you done to me?"

Only the echo of the dragons 'heartbeats answered her—slow, fading, and ominously uncertain.

* * *

The day began with silence.
Even the wind held its breath over the Vale of Embers, where the trees bled silver sap and the air tasted faintly of smoke. Lyra had wandered for hours—following whispers she couldn't name.

Her amulet, the one that shimmered like molten glass when she touched it, had burned against her chest since dawn. Each pulse drew her deeper into the wilderness, past ruins and riverbeds, until the valley opened beneath her feet.

That was when the sky moved.

At first, she thought it was a storm: a rolling wall of flame edged in gold.

Then wings broke through the smoke—enormous, radiant, cutting the sun in half. A dragon, alive and burning, spiraled down from the clouds, its shadow swallowing the valley whole.

Lyra fell to her knees, breath stolen. She had never seen such a creature except in dreams. Its scales gleamed like hammered sunlight; its eyes, molten amber, searched the ground below.

Then she saw him.

A figure astride the dragon's neck, black hair whipping in the wind, violet eyes glinting like tempered steel. His wings—ruined but radiant—shimmered faintly in the wake of the dragon's flight.

He wasn't human. He couldn't be.

Her heart stuttered. "A fairy… riding a dragon?" she whispered.

The dragon's roar split the air, deep and resonant. Dust and light scattered as it landed, talons carving molten grooves into the earth. The figure dismounted with the grace of a falling shadow, cloak rippling behind him.

Lyra stepped backward, instinctively raising her hand. Flame flickered along her fingers—unbidden, frightened.

He saw. And instead of drawing a blade, he froze.

The dragon bent its great head low, nostrils flaring. A soft glow rose between them, gold answering gold—the same energy that thrummed beneath Lyra's skin.

"She carries fire," the dragon said, its voice echoing in her mind.

"I feel it too," the fairy replied quietly. "But not dragonfire. Something… blended."

Lyra's pulse thundered. "Who are you?" she demanded. "And what are you doing here?"

The fairy inclined his head slightly. "My name is Riven," he said, voice low, almost a growl softened by centuries of restraint.

"And this is Auren. We meant no harm."

"Dragons rarely land without reason," she said.

Auren's eyes glimmered. "Nor do Emberwings flare their power at strangers."

She stiffened. "How do you—"

"Because your flame sings," Riven said simply. "It woke us."

Lyra's amulet pulsed again, and light spilled from her chest, washing across the clearing. The air filled with motes of silver fire that circled both dragon and fairy.

For a heartbeat, the three stood connected by threads of gold and starlight—dragon, fairy, shapeshifter.

In that instant, Lyra knew things she could not explain: The pain that lived behind Riven's eyes, the warmth of Auren's ancient heart, and the truth that the same flame burned within her veins.

The bond flared—and the ground shuddered as something vast stirred beneath it.

The sky dimmed. Shadows crept along the horizon like a tide of smoke.

Riven's hand went to his sword. "Shadowborn," he murmured. "They've found us."

Lyra's fire answered his fear, blazing up her arms. "Then let's make sure they regret it."

Auren's wings snapped open, sending sparks into the twilight.

"At last," the dragon rumbled. "Three flames against the dark."

Riven leapt onto Auren's back and extended a hand toward her. "If you stay here, they'll consume you. Come."

Lyra hesitated only a breath. Then she took his hand. The moment their fingers touched, fire wrapped around them both. She felt the ground vanish, the rush of wind, the burn of freedom.

The world fell away beneath them—trees, rivers, the ruined valley—until only sky remained.

Auren roared, wings slicing the storm apart, and Lyra's laughter rose with the wind, wild and bright.

"I've got you," Riven shouted over the roar.

"No," she answered, eyes blazing. "I've got you."

They flew until dusk, until the stars began to bloom. Below them, the world looked fragile, beautiful, alive.

Riven glanced back once, studying her face in the dragonlight. The wind tangled her hair, and the fire in her eyes was brighter than any dawn.

"She's the one, Firebound," Auren murmured in thought.

"I know," Riven replied. "The Emberwing has come."

Lyra met his gaze. "What did you say?"

But he only smiled faintly, as if afraid that speaking too soon might break the spell.

Above the clouds, three hearts beat in rhythm—one of flame, one of light, and one of shadow, learning to hope again.

And below, far beyond their sight, the Shadowborn began to gather.

CHAPTER FOUR:
Fire in the Storm

Night fell too fast.

One moment, the sky burned orange and violet, the next it was swallowed by shadow. The stars above the clouds flickered and went out, one by one, as though unseen hands were snuffing them.

Auren's wings faltered midbeat. "Something follows," he growled.

Riven felt it too — a chill in his bones, a hum in the air like a thousand voices breathing his name.

"Shadowborn," he said grimly.

Lyra turned. Behind them, the clouds convulsed — black mist boiling into shapes with glowing, hollow eyes.

They came like a storm of smoke and glass. Wings of darkness. Voices like broken flutes.

"Return the flame… return the light…" they whispered.

Auren roared and dove. Fire spiraled from his jaws, carving molten paths through the dark. The heat seared Lyra's face, but she didn't look away.

One Shadowborn reached them — a figure with wings made of shredded mist. It lunged at Riven, claws like shards of night.

He met it with his Veilblade, steel singing as it met shadow. The creature shrieked, splitting apart into ribbons of smoke.

"More coming!" Lyra cried.

"Then burn them!" Riven shouted.

"I don't know how!"

"Then feel it," Auren thundered. "The fire already knows you."

The amulet at her chest pulsed. Once. Twice. Then it exploded with light.

Flame poured from her hands — silver and gold, twisting together like living stars. It didn't scorch; it sang. The sound rang through the air, and the shadows recoiled.

Riven turned mid-strike, momentarily stunned. "By the Veil…"

Auren's scales flared brighter, feeding on her light.

"Her flame is ours, Firebound. She carries both starlight and fire!"

Lyra raised her palms toward the largest of the Shadowborn. "Leave us!" she cried.

The creature laughed — a hollow, echoing mockery. "You carry what we were denied. Give it to us, child."

Her fire answered for her.

It surged outward in a blinding arc, colliding with the Shadowborn midair. The explosion ripped open the clouds, lightning crackling through the wound.

When the light faded, the creature was gone — nothing left but drifting ash that sparkled like snow.

The force threw Lyra backward off Auren's spine. She screamed as the sky dropped beneath her — endless black, the ground still miles below.

"Lyra!" Riven's shout ripped through the wind. He dove after her, wings flaring uselessly, the broken light of them straining to catch her before the fall could claim her.

Auren twisted downward in a spiral, tail cutting through the air like a whip.

At the last moment, fire erupted from Riven's scars — his broken wings blazing whole for the first time in centuries. He caught her, pulling her against his chest, their flames merging mid-descent.

They hovered, weightless in a cocoon of light.

"You flew," she whispered.

"So did you," he said, breathless. "Together."

They landed in a valley of scorched grass. Auren folded his wings, smoke curling from his nostrils. The air was still trembling from the magic.

Riven set Lyra down gently. She was trembling, eyes wide, flame flickering across her fingertips like a heartbeat.

"I didn't mean to—"

"You did what none of us could," he said. "You ended a Shadowborn."

Auren bowed his great head, lowering his golden eyes to meet hers.

"Your fire carries both realms. It could heal the Veil… or break it forever."

Lyra swallowed hard. "Then we'd better make sure it's the first one."

Riven smiled faintly, weary but alive. "Welcome to the war, Emberwing."

Above them, the night slowly repaired itself — stars flickering back to life.

But far beyond the horizon, deep in the Voidlands, something vast and unseen stirred — the Night Sovereign, first of the Shadowborn, its voice rippling through the dark:

"The flame awakens. The hunt begins."

CHAPTER FIVE:
The Cavern of Echoes

Auren banked low, wings slicing through mist. The valley narrowed into a fissure of stone, half hidden by ivy and shadow. At the end of it, a waterfall poured in silver ribbons, its spray steaming against the dragon's warmth.

Riven touched Lyra's shoulder. "Hold on. This is no ordinary cave."

Auren folded his wings and slipped through the waterfall's veil. The crash of water gave way to silence—an immense chamber lit only by veins of molten rock winding through black stone. Their glow painted the walls in gold and amber, flickering like the breath of sleeping fire.

"My lair," Auren said, his voice echoing off the stone. "Hidden from both flame and shadow since the war of the Veil."

Lyra stared in awe. The floor shimmered with tiny scales embedded in the rock; the air tasted faintly of smoke and honey.

"It's beautiful," she whispered.

"It's home," Riven said quietly, sliding down from Auren's shoulder. "Or what's left of one."

They built a small fire in a hollow near the dragon's flank. Auren curled himself into a crescent around them, his breathing deep and steady, heat rolling off him in gentle waves.

Riven moved stiffly, his newly re-ignited wings dimming to faint glows along the scars. Lyra noticed the way he winced when he tried to fold them and the way he hid it with silence.

"You shouldn't have dived after me," she said softly.

"And let you fall?" His smile was crooked. "I've done enough falling for one lifetime."

31

She laughed—a quiet, tired sound—and sat beside him. The flames between them flickered strangely, silver and gold mingling with crimson. For a heartbeat, the fire took the shape of two wings twined together, then scattered into sparks.

When Riven reached to feed the fire, his hand brushed hers. The flame leapt higher.

A golden light coiled from her wrist, meeting the violet shimmer that pulsed along his scars. They twined in the air, a living thread of heat connecting them.

Auren lifted his head, one golden eye half-open.

"Your flames resonate," he rumbled. "Two halves of the same breath."

"Is that dangerous?" Lyra asked.

"Only if you deny it," said the dragon.

Riven drew his hand back slowly, the glow fading. "When your fire touched mine in the sky," he said, "I felt... whole. Not healed, not cursed. Just alive. It shouldn't be possible."

Lyra looked at her hands, still faintly luminous. "Maybe the fire knows something we don't."

A soft hum spread through the cave. From the far wall, a pattern of runes began to glow—ancient draconic script. Lyra rose, curiosity outweighing exhaustion.

The symbols rearranged themselves into light and sound, a whisper of old magic that even Riven seemed to half-remember.

"Two flames born apart shall meet, and the Veil shall tremble in their wake..."

The fire between them flared again, echoing the words.

Auren's voice joined the echo, low and solemn. "You are not

meant to stand alone, Emberwing. The fire that binds you both is the same that can mend the Veil—or burn it away."

Lyra turned back to Riven. "Then we'll have to learn which it is."

He met her gaze, eyes reflecting gold and silver. "Together," he said. "Until we know the truth."

The cave breathed with ancient warmth. Amber light danced along the crystal walls, reflecting streams of molten gold.

Far above, water dripped in slow, rhythmic patterns—soft enough to lull, steady enough to remind them the world existed beyond this refuge.

Auren lay curled around the fire pit in a great crescent of gold, his wings half-folded like a protective canopy. Heat from his scales radiated in waves, chasing away the cold that had followed them for days.

Lyra sat with her knees drawn to her chest, silver hair glowing in the firelight. Riven leaned beside her, his dark eyes softened by the warmth, the jagged scars at his back hidden beneath loose cloth.

Auren's enormous head lowered until he rested it on his forepaws, golden eyes flickering with memories far older than either of them could comprehend.

Riven looked up. "You've been quiet since the valley," he said, his voice low, almost respectful. "Something is troubling you."

Auren rumbled—not disagreement, not denial, but contemplation.

"Not troubling," he said. "Remembering."

Lyra tilted her head. "Remembering what?"

The dragon's gaze drifted to the fire, as though he saw through it—through the flame, through the stone, through time itself.

"When I was young," Auren murmured, "my elders used to tell a story.
A story so old it was carved into our bones before we hatched."

He breathed out, and the fire brightened, as though leaning closer to listen.

"It is the story of the First Flame. The story of Vaelrion."

Riven's breath caught.

Lyra's heart stilled.

Auren lifted his head slowly, his eyes radiant with ancient sorrow. "When the first dragons rose from the molten rivers of creation," Auren began, voice deep and reverent, "one among them burned brighter than all the rest."

Lyra drew in a slow breath, the words sinking into her bones.

"Vaelrion, the Eternal Flame," Auren continued. "His wings cast sparks that fell like comets. His shadow shaped mountains. His breath birthed oceans. And where his heartlight beat…magic itself awakened."

The fire reflected in Riven's violet eyes. He leaned forward slightly—as if hearing this for the first time in his life.

"He was the First Fire," Auren said softly. "The Dawn-Maker. Even the gods bowed to him."

The cave fell silent. Even the dripping water paused, as if listening to the dragon's tale.

Lyra's voice came out as a whisper. "What happened to him?"

Auren's gaze lowered. "Shadow," he answered. "And sacrifice."

He told them of the Hunger that rose where light did not reach.
Of the Shadowborn.
Of Vaelrion's endless war.
Of the moment he tore open his own heart to forge the Veil and save creation.

Lyra's throat tightened.
Riven's hands curled into fists.

"His flame," Auren said, "was not lost. It spread—to the stars, to magic, to us."

He turned his great head toward Lyra then, studying her glowing silver hair, the shimmer of flame beneath her skin. "And to you."

Her breath faltered. "M–me?"

"You carry what only one other has carried since the dawn," Auren said.

"A direct echo of the First Flame."

Riven looked at her sharply—pain, awe, and realization flickering across his expression like shifting firelight.

Lyra swallowed. "But I'm not a dragon."

Auren smiled faintly—a slow, ancient curl of smoke. "Fire chooses where it lives."

Riven stared into the fire, his voice barely audible. "Is that… how I freed you? How did the runes broke?"

Auren's eyes softened."Yes. Your spark was always there, Riven. Buried under frost. The moment you chose mercy over obedience… the flame answered."

Riven closed his eyes, jaw tight.

Lyra reached out, hesitating for only a heartbeat before placing her hand over his. He did not pull away.

Auren's warm breath flowed over them like a blanket.

"You both are pieces of an ancient fire," Auren murmured.

"And I will guard that flame with everything I am. Vaelrion gave his heart to save the world…and now, the world has given a piece of that heart to you."

Lyra leaned gently against Riven's shoulder. Riven exhaled slowly, letting the warmth settle into his bones.

The cave of echoes hummed around them—the same melody Vaelrion once breathed into the newborn world.

For the first time, they felt the truth of it:

They were no longer alone.

They were a flame reborn.

And the world was beginning to remember them.

The fire crackled lower now, glowing a deep molten orange. Auren shifted, unfolding one great wing and curling it more fully around Lyra and Riven. Heat radiated through the cavern like a steady heartbeat.

Lyra leaned closer.

Riven's eyes narrowed faintly, sensing the shift in Auren's tone.

The dragon inhaled as if drawing in courage from the stone itself.

"There is something else you must know," Auren said quietly. "A truth carried by dragons since the First Flame. A prophecy... spoken long before either of you drew breath."

Lyra tensed.
Riven's flame flickered beneath his skin.

"Prophecies," Riven murmured, "are often tools for tyrants."

"This one," Auren answered, "terrified tyrants."

He lowered his head, golden eyes glowing with reflected fire.

"When frost claims the sky and shadow steals the dawn, two flames divided shall rise as one. One born of memory. One born of mercy. And the dragon who remembers the First Light shall bind them together. They shall be Firebound. The last fire the world cannot unmake."

Silence.

Lyra stared at him, breath caught somewhere between fear and awe.

"Two flames divided...?"

"You," Auren said gently, turning to her. "And him."

Riven stiffened. "No. I am—"

"—one who chose mercy over frost," Auren said. "One whose heart answered fire with compassion. That has always been rarer than power."

Lyra touched her chest, feeling her fire pulse beneath her skin. "But why me?" she whispered.

"Because you are the flame of memory," Auren answered. "The last ember of the line the Fair Folk thought long dead."

Riven turned sharply toward her. "What line?"

Auren's gaze drifted to the flickering crystals along the cavern walls. "The line of Cyris. The Starborn King. The one who first shaped magic from Vaelrion's breath. His spark did not die—it merely hid. In your blood."

Lyra drew back, shaken.

Riven reached instinctively for her hand before he realized what he was doing. She didn't pull away.

Auren's voice softened.

"And together, you two awaken something the world has not seen since Vaelrion himself walked the heavens."

The flames settled to embers. Outside, the waterfall's murmur deepened into steady rain. Lyra lay against the warm curve of Auren's side, sleep tugging at her.

Across the fire, Riven watched her for a long moment, then closed his eyes. The faint light in his scars pulsed in rhythm with the glow at her throat.

Their breaths synced, their flames answering each other in dreams neither yet understood.

* * *

Far from the Cave of Echoes, beyond the reach of flame and frost, beyond the Veil's fragile shimmer, a deeper darkness stirred.

Not the soft kind that blankets sleeping forests. Not the quiet kind between stars.

A hungry darkness.

A wishing darkness.

A remembering darkness.

The Shadowborn Sovereign opened his eyes.

They were pits of shifting void—deep enough to swallow starlight. His crystalline throne pulsed with corrupted veins of cold blue fire. The air trembled as he inhaled.

"Flame..." His voice cracked like ice fracturing. "The ancient flame...stirs again."

He rose—slowly, as though the act angered gravity itself.

The chamber around him writhed.

Creatures formed from living shadow cringed at his feet, waiting.

"Two flames," he whispered. "One bright. One blackened. And the dragon who carries Vaelrion's dying song..."

His hand closed, twisting shadow into a spear of oozing obsidian.

"The Firebound live."

A tremor ran through the Shadowborn armies, a ripple of hunger and anticipation. He lifted his head toward the faint shimmering barrier of the Veil.

"The prophecy awakens," he hissed. "And with it... the end of the Veil."

The Sovereign smiled—a terrible, hollow shape.

"Find them. Bring me their fire. And let the world burn beneath my shadow once more."

The darkness swallowed his throne.

The hunt began.

The flames settled to embers. Outside, the waterfall's murmur deepened into steady rain. Lyra lay against the warm curve of Auren's side, sleep tugging at her.

Across the fire, Riven watched her for a long moment, then closed his eyes. The faint light in his scars pulsed in rhythm with the glow at her throat.

Their breaths synced, their flames answering each other in dreams neither yet understood.

CHAPTER SIX:
The Lesson of Flame

Night fell without stars.

The sky over the borderlands of Elderglen shimmered faintly, as though light was bleeding through thin silk. The trees along the edge of the mortal realm stood unnaturally still—branches frozen mid-sway, leaves suspended in a breath that refused to release.

Animals hid.
The wind fled.
The world waited.

A thin line of silver cut the darkness.
Not lightning.
Not magic.
Something older.

The Veil was trembling.

A whisper echoed through the trees—too soft for mortal ears, but sharp enough to slice through the silence.

"…open…"

The silver seam widened, cracking like a sheet of glass under pressure.

Light spilled out—not warm, not holy, but a cold radiance that made the shadows recoil.

Then came the second whisper:

"…free us…"

A pulse rippled outward from the Veil, bending the grass flat for miles.

The air thickened, heavy with frost, even though no clouds had formed and no winter wind blew.

41

The silver seam split.
Darkness poured through.

The first Shadowborn scout emerged as a shifting silhouette—humanoid only in the loosest sense. Its limbs stretched like smoke. Its head glimmered with faint veins of blue light, pulsing where a heart might once have existed. Its feet did not touch the earth.

The second scout followed, dragging a spear shaped from pure shadow, its tip dripping with something that did not fall, but clung to the air.

A third slithered forward, featureless except for its eyes—two dim coals lit by ancient hunger.

They halted just beyond the threshold. The trees around them withered, their bark blackening, their leaves curling inward as though recoiling in fear.

The first scout inhaled deeply, savoring the taste of the world. "Warm…" it whispered. "Too warm."

The second clicked its jaw, the sound like knuckles cracking underwater.

"The Sovereign was right. Flame rises again."

The third lifted its head toward the Cave of Echoes, hidden far beyond the mountains. "I smell it," it murmured. "Old flame. New flame. And something… forbidden."

The shadows quivered in anticipation.

The first scout extended its hand, fingers unraveling into tendrils of black smoke. They brushed the grass, leaving frost behind with every touch.

"Find the dragon," it said. "Find the Firebound."

The others stirred, their forms pulsing like wounded stars.

"And the girl?"

"The girl," the first scout whispered, "is not to be touched."

A shudder ran through all three.

"She belongs to Him."

They turned as one toward the mountains.

The shadows lengthened beneath their feet, merging into a single black river that flowed ahead of them like a living path.

Above them, the seam in the Veil sealed shut again with a soft hiss.

The breach was gone. But its presence lingered, like the aftertaste of poison.

The forest exhaled.

A raven dropped dead from its branch.

The scouts vanished into the darkness.

* * *

Morning came softly to the Cavern of Echoes. The waterfall's silver curtain scattered light through cracks in the stone, turning the air into ribbons of gold and mist. Auren's slow breathing rumbled like a forge at rest; each exhale carried the scent of rain and smoke.

Lyra woke first. Her hand drifted across the floor, tracing the faint cracks that glowed beneath the rock. They pulsed—once, twice—in time with her heartbeat.

"It is answering you," Auren said, opening one great eye. "Flame is a language. It listens before it speaks."

Riven stirred nearby, half-smiling. "And what exactly is it saying?"

"Many things. Watch."

The dragon inhaled, and fire shimmered over his tongue—shapes forming within it, curling like letters made of light. The cave walls mirrored the patterns, bright and fleeting.

"Each breath is a word," Auren explained. "A promise. A truth. You do not command flame—you speak it, and it answers if it finds your heart worth hearing."

Lyra tried to imitate the motion, focusing on the warmth rising in her chest. The flame she called was small but pure, a silver ribbon that spelled something she didn't understand.

"What did I say?" she asked.

Auren tilted his head, amused. "You said, 'I am listening. ' That is where every true fire begins."

Riven reached into the glow, tracing a faint symbol with the tip of his dagger. The mark flared violet, then faded.

"And that?" Lyra asked.

"My name," he said quietly. "Before the Queen took it."

The silence that followed was gentle, not heavy. The flames between them shifted again, joining their colors—his violet, her silver-gold—into a brief harmony. Even Auren seemed to watch without breathing.

A sudden chill swept the chamber. The waterfall's song changed pitch.
Riven's head snapped up. "Someone crosses the veil."

A shape emerged through the spray—a slender fairy armored in pale glass, wings trembling from the cold. The sigil of the Queen's Court gleamed on her breastplate. Her face was familiar, though thinner now.

"Ser Calith," Riven said, rising. "I thought you were dead."

"Exiled," she answered, voice shaking. "They sent me to find you. The Court is dying, Riven. The Shadowborn breach the lower groves. The Queen—" she hesitated, glancing at Lyra and the dragon—"the Queen demands your return."

"Demands?" Auren's growl rolled through the cavern. "After tearing his wings?"

Calith flinched but stood firm. "She says the war cannot be won without the Firebound. Without her." She looked at Lyra with awe and fear mingled. "The Emberwing walks the mortal sky. The prophecy moves."

Lyra's heart thudded. "If she knows I exist, she'll try to use me."

Riven sheathed his blade slowly. "Then we go on our terms, not hers."

Auren's eyes burned like sunrise. "To walk into the Queen's Court again is to tempt death."

"Maybe," Riven said. "But if the Veil is breaking, we can't hide here forever."

The morning light barely reached the mouth of the Cave of Echoes where they stood, dawn spilling through the waterfall. Mist curled across the forest floor, faintly glowing where it drifted through veins of ancient stone. The fire-runes along the walls dimmed one by one as if bowing farewell.

Lyra tightened the strap of her cloak and stepped toward the waiting dragon with a determined glint in her silver eyes.

Auren lowered his massive head, nostrils humming with quiet approval.

Riven watched her from the side, the breeze tugging at the dark edges of his hair. His expression was unreadable at first — part

45

worry, part pride, part something deeper he had not yet learned how to name.

Lyra turned to him and spoke with a steadiness that surprised even herself. "Teach me more of the flame on the way and of Valerian," she said. "If I must face a queen, I want to speak in the language her fear forgot."

Auren rumbled in warm amusement. "You speak boldly for one so young."

"Boldness is all I have," Lyra said. "And fire. Even if I don't understand it yet."

Riven stepped closer, meeting her gaze head-on. "Understanding will come. The fire inside you listens before it speaks. You simply need to know how to hear it."

Lyra drew a breath that tasted of morning frost and dragon heat. "Then teach me."

Riven's eyes met hers across the dragon's scales. "Whatever happens, we stay together."

"Until the stars fall," she said.

Auren unfurled one wing in invitation, his golden scales catching what little sun pierced the trees.

"Climb," he said gently. "We ride toward the Frostlight ruins.
And while we fly... I will teach you the tongue of flame."

Lyra mounted first, settling just behind the ridge of Auren's blazing shoulders. Riven swung up after her, sitting close enough that she could feel the warmth radiating through him—a warmth that was not wholly of dragonfire.

And as Auren leapt into the open sky, the waterfall burst into steam behind them—fire meeting water, light meeting shadow—heralding the alliance the world had not seen since the age before the Veil.

Lyra gasped.

The world dropped away beneath her, the forest shrinking into a tapestry of gold and green. Wind tugged at her hair, carrying the scent of smoke and cloud.

Auren's voice rolled through their minds as the air thinned.

"The first rule of flame: Fire remembers."

Lyra closed her eyes, listening.

"It remembers its source," Auren said. "Its shape. Its purpose. Its name."

Riven added softly: "And it remembers those who carry it."

Her chest tightened. She looked down at her hands, feeling faint warmth flicker beneath her skin.

Auren continued: "Vaelrion spoke not with words, but with intention. With truth made visible. With light shaped into meaning."

Lyra leaned forward instinctively. "And can I speak like that?"

Auren's eye swiveled toward her, gleaming. "You already do. Every time you choose truth. Every time you refuse to let fear shape you."

He turned his great head back toward the horizon.

"But if you wish to speak as Vaelrion spoke...you must first learn to ignite without burning."

Lyra's breath caught. "Teach me."

Auren's chest expanded, and a soft ripple of gold shimmered across his scales. "Repeat after me," he said. "The first word is Aesh'lan."

The sound vibrated through the air like a warm tremor — not spoken, but felt.

Lyra tried to mimic the rhythm. Her first attempt came out thin. Her second, broken. But her third—

Her third sparked.

A faint curl of gold rose from her throat, drifting like smoke caught in amber light.

Riven inhaled sharply.

Auren's approval warmed the air.

"Good," the dragon said. "Very good."

Lyra stared at the tiny flame she had shaped with breath and sound alone. "What does it mean?"

Auren's voice softened. "It means I am not afraid."

Riven's gaze lingered on her for a long moment, something unspoken flickering behind his black eyes.

Lyra swallowed, repeating the word under her breath until it steadied her heartbeat.

"Aesh'lan," she whispered. "I am not afraid."

Auren rumbled.

"The Frostlight Queen will not know what to do when she hears you speak it. Flame was the one language she tried to erase."

Lyra lifted her chin, staring toward the pale line of mountains in the distance. "Then let her hear it."

* * *

In the place where the Veil had cracked, frost spread across the earth like veins.

48

The Shadowborn scouts lifted their heads.

They had heard the dragon take flight. They had felt the flicker of ancient flame.

And now— as Lyra spoke the first word of the First Flame in centuries—a tremor rolled through the Veil like distant thunder.

The Sovereign's voice clawed through the darkness. "Find her."

The ground froze. The shadows lengthened.

"Bring me the girl…and the knight whose heart betrays him."

The hunt accelerated.

CHAPTER SEVEN:
The Shattered Gates of Elderglen

The skies changed as they flew.

On the first day, the world below them was green — forests sweeping like ocean waves, rivers glinting in sunlight. Auren's wings beat steadily, each stroke a rhythmic comfort.

Lyra spent those hours learning new flame-words, her voice growing steadier, her fire answering more quickly.

Riven answered her questions when she asked. But he grew quieter. He watched the horizon more than he watched her. Each league nearer to Elderglen tightened something inside his chest.

DAY TWO:

Clouds gathered low and pale. The air grew colder, and the wind tasted faintly of frost.

Lyra noticed Riven's posture stiffen when the first hints of the Frostlight realm appeared — crystalline ridges, silver trees with bark that shimmered unnaturally.

She touched his arm gently. "You're… not speaking much."

His jaw tightened, though he kept his gaze forward, black eyes fixed on the distant gleam of Elderglen's ruined towers.

"The Frostlight Queen was not kind to trespassers," he said finally. "Or to those who disappointed her."

Lyra studied him. His scars burned faintly through his shirt — white, cold, memories etched into skin. The wind blew through the torn remnants of where his wings once had been.

"Are you afraid?" she asked softly.

Riven inhaled sharply. He glanced away. "Fear is not something knights admit to."

"You're not a knight anymore," she whispered. "You are something far stronger."

For a heartbeat, he almost smiled — a flicker of warmth behind the darkness. But then the wind shifted, carrying the faintest trace of frost and memory.

His smile died.

"You do not understand what she can take from someone," he murmured.

"What she took from me."

Auren's voice drifted through their minds, calm and steady. "She cannot harm you now. Not while you are Firebound. Not while I still breathe."

Riven didn't answer.

Because Riven feared something Auren's fire could not protect: facing who he once was.

Nightfall — Day Two

They camped on a mountain ledge beneath sheltering stone. Auren curled around the entrance, creating a warm cavern with his body.

Lyra slept tucked between the dragon's foreleg and Riven's side.

Riven didn't sleep.

He sat awake long into the night, staring at the icy glow on the horizon.

Lyra stirred eventually, blinking sleepily. "You're awake."

He exhaled. "Couldn't sleep."

She sat beside him, pulling her cloak around her shoulders. "Tell me why you fear her."

Silence. The fire crackled softly behind them.

Riven flexed his hand — and for the smallest instant, flame flickered across his palm, then died.

"Because I loved her once," he said quietly. "Not as a man loves a woman. But as a soldier loves a commander. As a son loves the idea of a mother."

Lyra's heart ached at the tremor in his voice.

"She taught me to fly," he whispered, eyes glistening. "She crowned me with frostlight. She told me I was born for greatness."

His throat tightened.

"And when I became something she didn't understand…she tore me apart rather than admit she was afraid."

Lyra reached for his hand again. This time, he let her take it.

"You don't owe her anything," she said softly.

He closed his eyes. "I owe her my fear."

Day Three

By the third day, the landscape had transformed completely.

Frostlight crystal spires rose like broken teeth from the earth. Pale mist curled around the ruins, swirling in unnatural patterns. Auren's wings beat harder as the wind thickened, heavy with magic.

Lyra felt Riven stiffen behind her.

"We're close," he murmured.

Auren's voice vibrated beneath them. "The Queen feels your return. Her throne remembers you."

Lyra swallowed. "And you?"

Riven's pause was long. Then, barely above a whisper: "I don't know if I'm ready."

Auren's golden eye turned back toward him, warm and fierce. "Then be afraid. But fly anyway. Fear is not your chain —it is your fire's first breath."

Lyra reached back, taking Riven's hand again. "You are not alone."

He closed his fingers around hers — slowly, almost reverently.

For the first time in three days, he looked away from the horizon.

"No," he said softly. "Not anymore."

Auren let out a deep, rumbling growl of pride.

And together —
shapeshifter, fallen knight, and golden dragon —
they flew the last miles toward the Frostlight ruins…

…where the Queen waited
and the prophecy would begin to unfold.

Below, forests stretched to the horizon, their leaves made of glass and moonlight.

Lyra had imagined Elderglen as a place of music and wonder. Instead she found silence. No birds sang. The air shimmered with the residue of old spells, and the trees bled white sap from wounds that would not heal.

"It wasn't always like this," Riven said quietly from Auren's back. "The Queen's magic holds the realm together—but she's draining it faster than the land can breathe."

"She's dying," Calith said from behind them, her armor dulled by travel. "And with her, everything else."

Auren's great wings beat slower. "I can smell it," he rumbled. "Rot beneath perfume. Decay wrapped in starlight."

They reached the border at dusk. Once, the Gates of Elderglen had been carved from living crystal, their towers crowned with singing lights. Now the towers leaned, half-melted, and the song was gone—only a low hum that made the air ache.

At the gate waited a company of sentinels—fairy knights in pale silver mail. When they saw the dragon descending, they raised spears that flickered with spell light.

"Hold," Riven warned. "Do nothing unless I ask."

Lyra's pulse quickened as Auren landed, dust and glass swirling around them. The captain stepped forward, helm hiding his face.

"Riven of the Fallen Wing," he said, voice like brittle ice. "The Queen commands your surrender."

Riven slid from Auren's side. His tone was calm but his eyes burned

"I no longer serve her command. I come under my own banner—seeking parley."

"And the creature?" the captain demanded, nodding toward Lyra. "She bears flame forbidden by decree."

"She bears the hope you've forgotten," Riven answered.

The air cracked. Magic shimmered between the guards as they whispered spells of restraint, but before they could speak again, a new voice cut through the tension—soft, measured, unmistakably royal.

"Let them pass."

The guards parted. A carriage of glass and bone glided forward, drawn by spectral stags. Within it sat Queen Aislyn, her beauty as cold as the moon reflected in water. Her wings, once bright, were translucent and veined with darkness. Every breath she took left frost in the air.

"My exile returns," she said. "And brings the fire I forbade."

"Your realm is dying," Riven said. "You need what we carry."

The Queen's gaze shifted to Lyra. For a heartbeat, her mask of serenity cracked; the faintest flicker of fear—or awe—crossed her face.

"So the Emberwing is real."

"Real enough to end the Shadowborn," Lyra said, surprising herself with the steadiness in her voice.

"Or to end us all," the Queen replied. "Bring them to the Court. Let the Veil decide."

They rode beneath arches once alive with magic. Now each shimmered only faintly, reflecting memories of what had been: fountains frozen mid-song, gardens of crystal wilted to dust. Fairies watched from balconies, silent, eyes hollow with wonder and fear.

Lyra felt their thoughts pressing against her mind—curiosity, envy, terror. Her fire stirred uneasily beneath her skin.

"They think I'm a weapon," she whispered.

Riven looked at her. "So did I, once."

Auren's low voice joined them. "Then teach them you are more than fire. Teach them to listen."

They reached the inner citadel as night settled. The Queen's Hall rose from the heart of the city, a spire of glass crowned with pale flame. Inside, the air was bitterly cold. Every surface gleamed—beautiful, dead.

The Queen dismounted her carriage and turned toward them, her guards forming a circle.

"The Shadowborn grow stronger," she said. "They have breached the first rings of the Veil. I will not see my realm devoured. If your power can mend the rift, Emberwing, you will do it—or the Veil will feed on you instead."

Lyra met her gaze. "And if it's your magic that keeps it broken?"

A murmur rippled through the court. Riven stepped closer to her, hand on his sword. Auren's talons clicked against the floor, smoke curling from his nostrils.

"Careful," the Queen warned. "You stand in the heart of my power."

"No," Riven said quietly. "We stand in the shadow of your fear."

The frostlight trembled. For the first time in an age, warmth spread through the hall—the subtle shimmer of Lyra's flame brushing against the dying magic of the Queen's. The walls groaned, ancient spells creaking awake.

Outside, thunder rolled across the Veil.

CHAPTER EIGHT:
The Shadowborn Strike

A pulse. A faint, cold tremor underfoot.

Auren froze. "Do not move."

Lyra stiffened.
Riven's hand went to the hilt of his blade.

The frost at their feet cracked—
once,
twice,
three times.

Not from cold. From movement.

A hiss tore through the silent air. Then the frost erupted.

Shadowborn scouts burst from beneath the ice, their forms rippling between solid and smoke. Three. Six. Twelve.

Riven shoved Lyra behind him. "Auren—!"

A giant shadow slammed into Riven before he could finish the warning.

He crashed backward into a column of frostlight crystal, the impact exploding light across the courtyard.

Lyra screamed his name.

Riven staggered to his feet, vision swimming.

One of the creatures loomed over him—taller than the others, its body carved from obsidian darkness, its eyes two cold blue embers.

It spoke.

Not to Auren.
Not to Lyra.

To him.

"The fallen knight," it whispered. "The one who survived the fire."

The creature stepped closer, tendrils stretching toward his throat. "Give him to the Sovereign," it crooned. "He will burn so beautifully."

Riven froze. His heart hammered once — hard — against his ribs. Not from fear of death. But from the terrible recognition of those words.

The Sovereign did not want him destroyed.

The Sovereign wanted him *burning*. Alive.

Auren roared behind him, but Shadowborn chains forced the dragon down, pinning his wings to the frostbitten ground. Lyra's flame guttered as dark mist curled around her, dimming her light.

Riven stood alone.

Surrounded.

Unarmed.

Unready.

But—

Something inside him stirred.

The Shadowborn loomed over him, its eyes glowing with cold blue veins of hunger. Its tendrils brushed his neck. Frost crawled across his skin.

He could feel it —the Sovereign's will, sliding across his thoughts like a cold hand.

"Your fire is fractured," the creature whispered. "Broken. Beautifully broken."

Riven's breath caught. His fire?

He had no fire.
He had frost.
He had pain.
He had scars and silence and a name that no Court wanted spoken.

A pulse of heat. A flicker. A memory of dragonfire shattering chains in the darkness.

His vision blurred—then sharpened—as gold light ignited beneath his skin.

The Shadowborn reached for him—The tendril tightened around his throat. "The Sovereign will remake you in shadow. He will shape your flame to his purpose."

Riven's pulse stuttered.

Flame. The word struck him like lightning.

He opened his mouth, desperate for air—and instead of breath, something *else* stirred. A spark. A memory. Not his.

And Riven's flame answered.

It burst from him in a ring of gold and red, pure and bright as the heart of a sun. The blast sent the nearest creature screaming backward, its form disintegrating like burning fog.

Lyra gasped.

Auren's chains shattered in a distant echo —as if the moment Riven touched the flame inside, the world reacted.

Riven stared at his hands, horrified and awed. Golden fire crackled along his skin, pulsing in thin lines like ancient runes awakening.

"What—what is this?" he whispered.

Auren's voice thundered with shock. "Riven… that is Vaelrion's fire."

The largest Shadowborn screamed, its tendril recoiling. "Impossible! He bears no dragonblood!" Its voice cracked. "No…No. You should not—"

More flames erupted — Riven's flames — but unlike Lyra's bright core-fire, this blaze carried a darker undertone, a fierce and ancient pulse, as if something deep within him had been waiting centuries for this moment.

The Shadowborn recoiled in violent terror.

"The Broken Flame!" one shrieked. "The Sovereign warned us of him!"

Riven turned, eyes like burning gold.
The frost under his feet began to melt.
Lyra's voice called his name — faint, terrified.

But he couldn't answer.

Something ancient roared awake inside him.

Something hot.
Something bright.
Something that had been waiting, sleeping beneath his frost and fear and grief.

His heart pulsed—

Once. Twice. A third time — and then the fire erupted. For the first time in his life—he wasn't afraid.

Golden flame tore from his chest like a sun being born.

The blast of heat cracked the frostlight pillars, shattered the frozen courtyard, and hurled the nearest Shadowborn into the air, its scream dissolving into smoke before it hit the ground.

A second wave burst from his hands, uncoiling in ribbons of molten light that chased away the shadows clawing for Auren and Lyra.

And the Shadowborn fled.

Riven staggered forward, stunned, staring at his own hands as gold fire danced along his skin, pulsing in patterns like ancient runes.

Lyra gasped.

Auren rose behind them, completely free now, wings unfurled to their full glory.

The surviving Shadowborn scrambled backward, screeching.

"The Broken Flame lives!"
"The Sovereign warned us!"
"We cannot face him—RUN!"

Their shadows unraveled, fleeing into the cracks of the ruin.

Silence followed.

Riven stood in the center of scorched frostlight, breathing hard, flame flickering across his skin like a heartbeat made visible.

Lyra approached slowly, eyes wide, voice trembling.

"Riven… that fire— it's not mine. It's not a dragon. It's something else."

Auren stepped beside them, bowing his great head as if in reverence.

"It is Vaelrion's fire," he said softly. "Long buried. Long forgotten. Alive again in you."

Riven swallowed, throat thick.

Lyra rushed toward him. "Riven—your eyes—your fire—"

He lifted trembling hands. Flame still danced there.
Golden.
Alive.
Ancient.

"I don't… understand."

Auren smiled — the kind of smile dragons only make when witnessing a miracle. He approached, tail curling around them protectively. "I do," the dragon said. "You were born with frost. You chose mercy. And the moment you freed me… You awakened something Vaelrion left hidden in the Fair Folk long ago."

Riven stared at Auren. "Hidden? In me?"

Auren nodded, voice soft and reverent. "You were never meant to be her weapon, Riven. You were meant to be his. You were never frostbound. You were never hers. You were made of fire from the beginning. You simply needed something worth burning for."

Lyra took his hand, gripping it tightly. "You are not what the Queen made you. You are not your scars. You are not your fall."

She lifted his hand, letting her silver light reflect in his new golden flame. "You are Firebound."

Riven swallowed hard, emotion choking him—fear, awe, disbelief, hope—
all warring in the space behind his eyes.

"Then let the Queen see what she tried to destroy."

And with Auren behind them, Lyra beside him, and Vaelrion's fire burning in his hands—

Riven walked toward the Frostlight throne.

CHAPTER NINE:
Riven confronts the Frostlght Queen

The Frostlight throne room shimmered with warped reflections.

Columns of ice arched overhead like frozen ribs, and the air hummed with the sharp scent of old magic.

Auren landed at the shattered steps, folding his wings.
Lyra slid down first — silver flame flickering faintly.
Riven hesitated, golden fire still humming under his skin.

The Queen sat upon her fractured throne, taller than any fairy, her crown a jagged circlet of frost and light. Her eyes narrowed the instant she saw him.

Riven stepped forward.

Her voice cracked like shattering crystal.

"You dare return."

Riven's jaw tightened. Golden flame flared along his fingers.

"I came for answers."

She rose from the throne, frost spilling from her feet. "You were cast out.
Your wings stripped. Your name erased."

Riven took another step, fire curling around his palm. "And yet... here I am."

A flicker — fear — crossed her face.

For centuries, Riven had bowed to her.

Now she bowed to him.

She gestured sharply. The frost around them dimmed as if obeying.

Her voice lowered. "There is a reason I tore your wings."

Riven's fire flared dangerously. "Say it."

The Queen exhaled — and her breath fogged with dread. "Your wings were changing."

Riven blinked. "Changing?"

"Turning gold."

The throne room fell silent.

The Queen continued, trembling: "Only one being ever bore golden wings.

Vaelrion's chosen. The Flamebound."

She pointed at him. "You were becoming a vessel for the First Fire."

Riven staggered.

Lyra's hand caught his arm.

The Queen's voice cracked. "I feared you. I feared the prophecy. I feared the fire waking in you. So I took your wings before it could finish."

Riven's flame surged, golden and furious. "You mutilated me because you were afraid?"

The Queen bowed her head — for the first time in her reign. "Yes."

Riven's fire roared.

But Lyra stepped in front of him, silver flame matching his gold. "Riven," she whispered, "you are more than what she feared."

His fire dimmed... but only enough to keep the frost from melting.

* * *

Far beneath the Veil, in the throne of shadows, the Sovereign's eyes snapped open.

The three surviving scouts knelt — trembling, half-melted from Riven's fire.

One croaked out the words: "The Broken Flame... lives."

The Sovereign rose so slowly the shadows bent in agony around him. "Impossible."

The smallest scout lifted its head. "He bears Vaelrion's fire."

Silence.

Then—

The Sovereign laughed.

It was not a sound meant for living ears. It scraped across the air like a blade dragged over stone.

"Then the age of prophecy begins." He leaned forward, voice dripping with hunger. "Find him. Break him. Bring me the flame he guards."

The Void trembled.

Thousands of Shadowborn stirred.

The hunt became a war.

CHAPTER TEN:
Riven's First Full Battle With the Flame

The throne room doors shattered.

Shadowborn soldiers poured through — dozens, then hundreds —shapes of pure night, crawling across frost and fire alike.

Auren roared, unleashing a column of dragonfire.

Lyra shifted into white-hot flame, her wings unfurling in a blaze of silver.

Riven stepped ahead of them both.

The first Shadowborn lunged.

Riven drew a breath——and the fire answered.

Golden flame erupted from his body in a spiraling burst, forming a molten sigil beneath his feet. The blast tore through the first wave of Shadowborn, burning holes through their forms.

He moved like a comet tearing across the sky.

One strike — a spear of flame.
Another — wings of fire burst from his back, not flesh but light.
A third — a shockwave cracked the floor, sending enemies tumbling.

Riven roared: "You took my wings—now watch me fly without them."

He blasted upward, fire wings flaring wide, carving through the Shadowborn like sunrise through fog.

Auren stared upward in awe. "Vaelrion help us," he whispered. "He was meant for this."

Lyra's flame surged to join his.

Their fires intertwined — gold and silver — forming the first Firebound blaze the world had seen since creation.

The Shadowborn recoiled, shrieking.

The Frostlight Queen fell to her knees, eyes wide with terror—not at Riven's power…

…but at the prophecy unfolding before her.

Riven landed, fire simmering along his skin, eyes glowing like molten suns.

He turned to Lyra and Auren. "This is only the beginning."

Shadowborn filled the hall like a moving storm. The air crackled with frost and darkness, the walls closing in beneath their assault.

Lyra stepped beside Riven, her breathing steady despite the chaos. Her silver fire flickered along her arms — bright, sharp, controlled.

Riven's flame crackled gold at his fingertips — fierce, ancient, unpredictable.

He met her gaze. "Together."

She nodded.

They reached for each other — a simple, instinctive movement — and the moment their hands touched, the world *changed*.

Light erupted.

Not gold.
Not silver.

Both.

A dual blaze, swirling upward in a spiral of molten white fire. The brightness cracked the frostlike pillars and rippled through the throne room, scattering Shadowborn like sparks in a gale.

Their flames intertwined in perfect rhythm.

Riven's fire surged in raw bursts
— Lyra shaped it into spiraling arcs.
He unleashed ancient power
— she controlled its direction.
He burned bright
— she burned true.

Auren watched, stunned. "Firebound," he whispered. "Vaelrion's heart reborn... twice."

Riven and Lyra moved as one.

Their flames sang.

The Shadowborn screamed.

The Frostlight Queen trembled.

And the prophecy bloomed like dawn breaking over a dead world.

When the last Shadowborn in the chamber dissolved into ash, the Queen staggered backward, clutching her chest.

Her frostlight crown flickered, dimming. Her breath came faint and heavy.

Riven approached her slowly, golden embers still drifting from his fingertips.

"You feared me," he said quietly. "You hurt me because of what you saw."

The Queen's voice cracked. "I saw your fate."

Lyra tensed.

Auren leaned in, eyes narrowing.

The Queen raised a trembling hand. "It is not *you* who will burn the world, Riven."

Riven's eyes sharpened. "Then who?"

Her gaze drifted to Lyra. "The girl."

Lyra stepped back as though struck. "What?"

The Queen coughed, frost drifting from her lips like blood. "You are the spark…but she is the wildfire."

Riven's jaw clenched. "You lie."

"I read the prophecy myself," the Queen whispered, collapsing to her knees.

"If she loses herself… if she falls to shadow or grief… the First Fire will consume everything."

Lyra stared at her hands, trembling. "I would never—"

"Intent is not always destiny," the Queen rasped. "Beware the Sovereign.

He knows her weakness."

Her eyes flicked to Riven. "And yours."

Then — with one last exhale of frostlight —the Queen's body dissolved into drifting snow.

Riven stood frozen, torn between rage, fear, and disbelief.

Lyra whispered, "I'm not a destroyer. I won't be.". He reached for her hand. "You won't."

But the words did not soothe the tremor deep in his flame.

CHAPTER ELEVEN:
The Sovereign Sends His Champion

In the Void beyond the Veil, the Sovereign watched through the eyes of his dying scouts.

He saw Riven ignited.
He saw Lyra blaze beside him.
He saw the Queen fall.

His form surged upward, shadows buckling like waves around him. "The Firebound lives!"

His whisper cracked the entire plane of shadow.

A figure stepped out of the darkness — tall, armored in obsidian, with burning blue sigils cut across its chest. A blade of night hung at its side.

It bowed deeply. "My Sovereign."

The Sovereign's gaze hardened. "Dravaryn."
His champion.
His executioner.
His firstborn shadow.

"Go to the mortal realm. Find the Broken Flame. Break him."

The champion's head tilted. "And the girl?"

A cold smile. "Bring her to me. Alive."

Placing his hand upon his heart — a gesture of devotion that extinguished the last sparks of the lesser shadows around them. Then he vanished.

And the Sovereign whispered: "Let the world remember fear."

⁜ ⁜ ⁜

Back in the Frostlight throne room, the air still shimmered with lingering heat.

Riven sat heavily on a fallen pillar, staring at the fire dancing along his skin.

Lyra hovered beside him, torn between awe and dread.

Auren crouched low, his eyes old and solemn.

Lyra looked at the dragon.

"Tell us the truth," she whispered. "What does his fire mean?"

Auren's voice vibrated with something like reverence.

"Riven carries Vaelrion's Echo."

Riven blinked. "My what?"

Auren's golden eyes softened. "When the First Flame shattered himself to create the Veil, his power split — some to dragons, some to the Fair Folk…and one spark went astray."

He looked directly at Riven. "Into you."

Riven shook his head. "I was born frostbound. I was—"

"No." Auren leaned closer. "You were born hidden. Protected. Fate wrapped your flame in frost so no one — not even the Queen — would sense it too soon."

Lyra breathed out softly. "He was meant to survive."

"He was meant to awaken," Auren corrected. "And now he has."

The dragon's gaze turned grim. "But the Golden Fire is not only power."

Riven's stomach twisted. "What else is it?"

Auren's answer was soft and devastating. "It is a promise. A price.

And a fate that may cost your life."

Silence.
Cold, heavy silence.

Lyra grabbed Riven's hand. "Then we face it together."

Riven swallowed hard.

For the first time since his wings were torn,
since his exile,
since the fire awoke within him…

He allowed himself to believe her.

* * *

The throne room had fallen silent except for the soft crackling of residual flame. Lyra stood before Riven, their hands still linked, their fires dim but pulsing like two hearts struggling to beat in harmony.

Auren watched them with nervous intensity.

"Careful," he warned. "Fusion is not simply power shared. It is identity entwined."

But Lyra didn't let go.

Neither did Riven.

For a moment, nothing happened.

Then—

Their flames flickered.
Gold and silver.
Separate.

Then the flickers synchronized.

One heartbeat.
Two.

The floor beneath them glowed faintly, frostlight giving way to molten gold-white light.

Auren whispered: "It's starting…"

Lyra breathed in.

Riven breathed out.

And their fires met.

The ground shook.

The air warped.

Power erupted not *around* them, but *between* them — a blinding fusion-light neither had ever felt before. Gold fire wove with silver flame, spiraling upward into a column that punched through the shattered roof and into the sky.

Auren shielded his eyes with a wing. "By Vaelrion…"

The fusion-fire roared like a living thing.
Reality shivered.
The frost in Elderglen melted, revealing glimmering runes hidden for centuries.

Then—
just as quickly—
the light collapsed inward, snapping out like a candle pinched shut.

Riven and Lyra staggered apart, both panting, flames dimmed to mere embers.

Lyra gasped.

"What… what *was* that?"

Auren lowered his wing slowly, eyes wide. "A warning."

Auren stepped closer, voice low, ancient, heavy.

"You must understand. The Golden Fire is unlike any other flame. It remembers everything."

Riven wiped sweat from his brow, trembling. "Remembers?"

"Every bearer. Every sacrifice. Every death."

Lyra swallowed. "Death?"

Auren nodded solemnly.

"The Golden Fire always chooses a mortal host…and it always consumes them."

Riven's breath caught.

Lyra paled.

Auren continued: "The stronger the fire becomes, the faster it burns through its vessel."

Riven stared at his hands, flames coiling faintly beneath the skin. "So using this power… kills me."

Auren lowered his massive head. "It is the price every Flamebound must pay."

Lyra grabbed Riven's wrist, panic in her voice. "No. No— there must be another way—"

Auren turned to her gently. "There is one. But it is worse."

Riven's voice was barely a whisper. "Tell us."

Auren closed his eyes. "If a Flamebound refuses the fire…it finds a new host."

Lyra's heart stopped.

He met her gaze.

"And it will go to the one closest to him."

She released Riven's wrist like she'd been burned. "Me…"

Auren nodded. "If Riven rejects his fire…you will inherit it."

Lyra's fire flickered violently.

Riven's breath shook.

Auren added quietly: "And the Golden Fire…would destroy you in days."

Lyra stumbled backward. "So either Riven dies…or I do."

Silence fell.

A cold, merciless truth.

CHAPTER TWELVE:
Dravaryn Arrives and delivers the Sovereign's first strike

A sound like cracking bone echoed through the throne room.

A portal of pitch-black shadow ripped open in the air, frost spiraling outward as the temperature dropped instantly.

Riven pushed Lyra behind him.

Auren snarled, wings flaring.

A tall figure emerged. Clad in obsidian armor. Runes glowing blue across its chest. Eyes hollow, burning with voidlight.

Dravaryn. The Sovereign's champion.

He surveyed the ruined hall with cold amusement. "So this is where you hide, Broken Flame."

Riven's golden fire ignited instinctively.

Dravaryn tilted his head, almost curious. "The Sovereign sends greetings.

And chains."

He moved — faster than sight.

His obsidian blade slashed through the air, its edge dripping shadow.

Riven barely blocked with a burst of flame — the impact sending him crashing into a frost pillar.

Lyra screamed his name.

Auren lunged, exhaling a torrent of dragonfire.

Dravaryn stepped through it untouched. "Dragonfire?" He smiled without warmth. "How quaint."

He backhanded Auren with a wave of shadow so dense it cracked the dragon's scales and threw him across the hall.

Lyra's fire exploded in her palms. "Stay away from them!"

Dravaryn's gaze sharpened. "Ah. The wildfire." His voice slithered with hunger. "The Sovereign will be pleased."

Lyra backed away, her fire trembling violently along her skin.

Riven pushed himself up, blood on his lip, flame sputtering. He saw her shaking. He saw her eyes. And in them—Fear. Not of Dravaryn. Of herself.

"Lyra," Riven rasped. "Look at me."

She didn't.

Her hands glowed too brightly. Her fire spiraled out of control.

"What if she was right?" Her voice broke. "What if my fire ends the world?"

Dravaryn's laugh echoed through the hall. "It will."

Riven roared in fury, lunging toward him—

—but stopped when Lyra cried out, clutching her head as silver flames surged uncontrollably around her.

"I can feel it—the fire doesn't want to stop—it wants to consume—"

Riven grabbed her shoulders. His golden fire flared, intertwining with her silver flame, grounding it. "Listen to me."

Her breath shuddered. "Riven—I'm afraid—I'm afraid of myself—"

He pressed his forehead to hers, flames touching without burning.

"Then let me be your anchor. Let my fire hold yours. Let us burn together before either flame destroys you."

Her trembling eased.

Dravaryn snarled. "Enough of this."

But it wasn't enough for Riven. He lifted Lyra's face with both hands, golden flame rising. "Lyra."

She met his eyes.

Two flames — one gold, one silver — aligned. The Firebound ignited.

A blast of white-hot fusion-light erupted, hurling Dravaryn backward in a shower of shattered frost, carving a crater into the throne room floor.

Auren lifted his head slowly, stunned. "They did it…"

Riven held Lyra's hand tightly. "We are stronger together."

Lyra's eyes burned bright and steady. "Then let's fight."

And for the first time—Lyra wasn't afraid. She believed in her fire.

Because Riven did.

The throne room trembled as the blast of Firebound fusion-light faded.

Lyra leaned on Riven, steadying her breath.

Dravaryn rose from the crater he had carved into the froststone floor, obsidian armor cracked, voidfire leaking from the fractures like burning ink.

He tilted his head, something like fascination in his hollow eyes. "Impressive. But you misunderstand one thing, Broken Flame."

His shadow expanded beneath him like a living creature. "I was not sent to kill you."

Riven stepped forward, golden fire igniting along both arms. "That's unfortunate."

Dravaryn moved.

He blurred—
no, *vanished*—
then appeared behind Riven, a blade of shadow sweeping in an arc that would have cleaved a lesser being in half.

Riven spun, fire bursting from his arm in a shield of molten gold.

The two forces collided.

Shadow screamed.
Flame roared.
The shockwave shattered every remaining Frostlight pillar.

Riven flew back, skidding across the frost floor—but he did not fall. He caught himself, wiped the blood from his lip, and smirked. "You're slower than you look."

Dravaryn's voidfire pulsed in irritation. "You will die slowly, then."

They clashed again.

Fire struck shadow.
Shadow swallowed flame.
Flame burned through void.

The air twisted around them — too hot for frost, too cold for fire — the collision of two ancient forces that should never meet.

Auren whispered to Lyra: "He is fighting without control. He will burn himself open."

Lyra's eyes widened.

And Dravaryn pressed harder.

As Riven staggered back from a brutal shadow strike, Dravaryn lunged for Lyra.

Auren roared, leaping between them, wings flaring open with blinding gold."You will not touch her!"

Dravaryn smiled. "I was hoping you'd say that."

The champion raised his hand.
Shadows wriggled, entwining, forming barbed spears that aimed straight for Lyra's chest.

Auren didn't hesitate.

He inhaled deeply—
far deeper than any normal breath—
his chest expanding, scales glowing white-hot.

Lyra recognized that glow. "Auren—no—That's—"

The dragon unleashed an ancient rite forbidden even among dragons:

A column of pure, searing dragonfire burst from his throat — not gold, not red, but *white*, radiant as a newborn star. The blast struck Dravaryn full-force, hurling him backward through three shattered walls and out into the open courtyard.

But the blast took its price.

Auren collapsed to one knee, breathing raggedly, smoke rising from cracked scales.

Lyra ran to him. "That rite burns the life-force— Auren, why would you—"

He lifted his head. "Dragons guard the Firebound. With tooth. With flame.

With life."

Riven froze mid-fight, fire dying against his skin.

Auren had burned himself for them.

Dravaryn rose again — slower this time, armor smoldering.

"Very well." His voice rattled with fury. "No more games."

Dravaryn stepped forward, dragging his blade across the ground.

Shadow bled from it in waves.

"You want truth?" he hissed. "Here it is."

He pointed at Lyra. "She belongs to the Sovereign."

Lyra recoiled as if struck.

Riven's fire exploded at his feet. "Liar."

Dravaryn laughed — a hollow, broken sound. "Ask her. Ask the flame in her bones who first shaped it."

Lyra felt a cold pull deep inside her core — a memory she had never known she carried.
A voice.
A whisper.

Shadow... before light.

Her breath stuttered. "What... what does that mean?"

Dravaryn lifted his blade. "She is the Sovereign's blood."

Everything fell silent.

Riven's golden fire flickered.

Lyra staggered backward, shaking her head. "No—I'm not—That's impossible—"

Auren's eyes widened. "Lyra… your flame… it is reacting—"

Her silver fire surged violently, crackling with streaks of blue-black shadow.

Dravaryn's smile widened. "She is the heir to the Shadowflame. The wildfire that will consume the world."

Lyra screamed, pressing her hands to her head as her flame spiraled out of control.

Riven sprinted for her—

—but too late—

a shockwave of unstable silver-and-black fire erupted outward, ripping the floor apart.

Auren shielded her with his wings.

Riven was thrown across the hall, slamming into the wall.

Dravaryn didn't even flinch. "Bring her to the Sovereign," he commanded the shadows. "Or watch her burn everything you love."

Riven roared.

Not in fury.

In fear.

Fear *for* her.

CHAPTER THIRTEEN:
Riven Nearly Burns Himself Out to Save Her

Lyra collapsed to her knees, screaming as her fire spiraled uncontrollably, black veins streaking the silver light.

Dravaryn raised his hand. Shadow closed around her throat.

Riven saw red. He didn't think. He ignited.

The Golden Fire flared so violently that Auren shouted in alarm.

"RIVEN—STOP—YOU'LL BURN YOURSELF ALIVE—!"

He didn't care. He couldn't care.

Riven hurled himself across the throne room, golden fire blazing from every pore, from every scar, from the very memory of every pain.

He struck Dravaryn like a meteor. The impact was thunder.

The shockwave cracked the castle walls. Fire and shadow burst into the sky.

Riven roared: "YOU WILL NOT TAKE HER!"

His fire burned brighter and brighter—
too bright—
too fast—

Auren's eyes widened in terror. "Riven—STOP—YOUR HEART—"

Riven didn't stop.

He didn't even hear him.

The Golden Fire surged to its peak, devouring everything in its path, including him.

Lyra screamed his name as he burned himself open—skin glowing, veins molten, flame searing through him with lethal speed—

He had seconds.

Maybe less.

And still he pressed Dravaryn back, forcing him to kneel, forcing him to falter—

Dravaryn snarled: "You would die for her?"

Riven's voice broke—"In a heartbeat."

His flame burst one last time—

—and his body collapsed.

Lyra caught him before he hit the ground.

Riven's chest flickered weakly. His flame guttered.

He whispered her name once—

and the fire went dark.

Riven lay limp in her arms.

His skin, moments ago molten with golden fire, had turned pale — almost translucent. His heartbeat was gone.

His chest was still.

His flame was out.

Lyra shook him, her breath frantic.

"Riven—RIVEN—please—!"

Silence.

Auren crawled toward them, dragging his injured body across the ruined throne room.

"Lyra… stop…" His voice trembled. "The Golden Flame has burned him empty. He cannot come back."

Lyra's tears hit Riven's cheek and hissed — tiny sparks bursting where they landed.

Her fire was leaking into him already.

And she knew exactly what she had to do. Even if it destroyed her, she pressed both hands to Riven's chest.

"Take it," she whispered. "Take my flame. Take all of it."

Silver fire erupted from her palms, pouring into his heart like liquid light.

Auren's eyes went wide with terror.

"LYRA—STOP—You will burn yourself—"

She didn't stop.

Her flame poured into him in torrents, lighting his veins with silver-white brightness. Her hands shook violently, her breath faltering as her own flame dimmed.

Riven's chest rose—once—

—and Lyra gasped with relief.

But then her vision blurred. Her knees buckled.

Auren roared: "Lyra—ENOUGH!"

But she whispered one final word into Riven's ear: "Come back to me."And she collapsed.

Dravaryn rose from the crater Riven had blasted him into, moving with silent fury. Voidfire flickered across his armor. His blade dripped shadow.

He did not look weakened.

He looked enraged.

He saw Lyra lying unconscious beside Riven, her flame flickering like a dying candle.

He smiled. "At last."

Auren lunged to protect them—but the champion raised one hand.

A prison of shadow slammed into place around the dragon, binding him in chains of frozen void.

Auren roared, flames erupting from his jaws —but nothing broke the chains.

They were forged by the Sovereign himself.

Dravaryn lifted Lyra effortlessly, cradling her unconscious body as if she weighed nothing. "You burn beautifully, little wildfire."

Auren thrashed, scales cracking. "DON'T TOUCH HER!"

Dravaryn turned his empty gaze toward the dragon. "You cannot stop what she was born to be."

He stepped into a rent in the air — a gash of pure shadow — and disappeared with Lyra in his arms.

The Veil sealed behind him.

Auren collapsed in chains, exhausted and bleeding golden ichor.

"Riven… please… wake up…"

* * *

Deep in the Void, the Sovereign paused mid-step. A tremor passed through him.

A flame — a very specific flame —flickered out.

He inhaled deeply, savoring the moment. "Ahhh… the Broken Flame dies."

The shadows around him erupted in whispers of triumph.

But then—

Something else.

A spark flared.
Gold mixed with silver.
A fusion pulse.

The Sovereign froze.

His eyes snapped open — pits of swirling void.

"Impossible."

He reached into the currents of fate and flame, tasting what remained of Riven's fractured fire.

Silver life-force.

Lyra's life-force.

"She gave herself to him…" He hissed with delight. "Of course she did."

A dark smile spread across his face. "Bring her to me. Now."

The shadows churned.

The war had begun.

87

CHAPTER FOURTEEN:
Auren Tries to Save Them Both

Auren strained against the Sovereign's chains until blood seeped from beneath his scales.

He crawled toward Riven's still body, dragging the chains like anchors behind him.

Riven lay unmoving.

No flame.
No heartbeat.

But Auren saw something the Sovereign had missed.

A faint glow — a soft curve of gold — pulsed once beneath Riven's skin.

Auren whispered urgently: "Riven… Riven, listen to me…"

The dragon pressed his forehead lightly to Riven's chest — a gesture of ancient dragon kinship.

"You must not die. Not now. Not when she needs you most."

Golden tears dripped from Auren's snout, sizzling where they hit the frost. "Lyra gave her flame to you…you must choose to live with it."

Nothing.

Auren's voice broke. "If you fade now, her sacrifice is wasted."

Still nothing.

The dragon trembled. "She is in the Sovereign's hands."

A spark.

Faint.

But real.

Auren gasped. "That's it —come back, Riven —FIGHT your way back!"

The fire inside Riven's chest pulsed again—
stronger—
brighter—
burning silver at the edges.

Auren laughed through tears of exhaustion. "Yes… yes… that's her flame…and yours…combined…"

The golden-silver fire surged.

Auren whispered the last truth, the one that would decide Riven's fate: "If you wake…she lives."

The flame erupted.

Riven gasped as his eyes snapped open —burning with gold and silver intertwined. Not gold. Not silver.

Both — swirling together like twin stars caught in orbit.

Auren staggered backward as Riven sat up, flame erupting from his body in a molten halo. The froststone beneath him cracked into glowing fragments.

His voice rasped like a forge coming alive: "Where is she?"

Auren exhaled shakily. "Dravaryn took her. Through the Veil."

Riven stood.

His wounds closed instantly.
His heartbeat thundered.
His fire rose without pain.

The new flame—the dual flame Lyra had given him— burned steady and bright.

But beneath the strength was a tremor of terror. "She's alone with him."

Auren nodded, wings drooping under exhaustion. "We must hurry.
But the Veil is closed. We cannot—"

Riven didn't wait.

He vanished.

One instant he was there—
the next he was streaking across the ruins like a meteor of fused gold and silver light.

He moved faster than ever before.
Because it wasn't only his flame driving him.

It was hers.

* * *

Lyra awoke to darkness.

Not the absence of light.
A presence.
A darkness that moved, breathed, whispered.

She tried to stand, but chains of living shadow held her suspended above a black, starless abyss.

A voice slid beside her ear. "Hello, little wildfire."

The Sovereign stepped from the void.

His form was both man and darkness — tall, robed in shadowflame, his eyes a bottomless void where stars went to die.

Lyra tried to ignite her fire.

Nothing.

Only a dull ache where her flame had been.

He smiled. "You gave your flame to him. How devoted."

Lyra snarled, struggling against the chains. "Get away from me."

The Sovereign studied her face.

"It is astonishing," he murmured. "The world finally produced a bearer capable of holding two powers: the First Fire…and the Shadowfire."

Lyra froze.

Shadowfire.

Her blood turned cold.

The Sovereign leaned close enough for her to feel his chill. "Did you truly think you belonged only to dragons and light? You are mine as well."

She spat the words: "I will never be yours."

His smile widened. "You already are."

The chains tightened until she screamed.

* * *

Back in Elderglen, Auren limped to the center of the ruined hall, blood trailing from cracked scales. He knew what he had to do. He also knew it was forbidden.

He planted his claws into the frost—drew in a breath so deep the hall trembled—and whispered the words no dragon had spoken since Vaelrion's sacrifice: "I invoke the Rite of Sundering Flame."

The air snapped.

Frost shattered.
Light warped.
Reality bent backward.

Auren's chest glowed white-hot again, hotter than any mortal flame should burn. His body convulsed with pain.

"Forgive me, Vaelrion…but they are my children."

He roared.

A tear ripped through the air—
a jagged wound of shimmering gold and black.
A gateway carved open by dragon wrath and ancient fire.

Auren collapsed, barely conscious.
His scales dimmed.
His breath faltered.

But he smiled weakly. "Go, Riven…save her…"

Riven appeared at the threshold—eyes blazing with the dual flame.

He didn't hesitate.

He dove into the tear.

The Veil screamed around him.

CHAPTER FIFTEEN:
Riven's Transformation into the True Firebound

The Shadow Realm swallowed him whole.

Cold.
Dark.
Endless.

But Riven did not dim.

His flame grew brighter.

He stepped onto the obsidian floor of the Sovereign's domain—and the ground cracked beneath his feet.

The air trembled.

A distant voice whispered: "…you are not meant to survive this…"

Riven ignored it.

His vision pulsed with silver threads—
Lyra's life-force calling to him like a beacon.

The fire inside him strained, surged—

—and snapped into its true form.

Flame wings erupted from his back.

Not frost remnants.
Not illusions.

Wings of molten light — gold and silver intertwined. The wings he should have been born with.

The wings the Queen feared.

The wings of Vaelrion.

Riven roared, the sound shaking the Shadow Realm.

He had become the thing of prophecy.

The true Firebound.

The Sovereign felt the shift. His smile faltered. "…No."

Riven stepped into the throne hall.
Flame swirling.
Eyes burning bright as twin suns.

"Let her go."

The Sovereign's shadows recoiled.
For the first time in eons—

—the darkness took a step back.

The throne hall of shadows stretched endlessly, carved from obsidian and living darkness. Lyra hung suspended in chains of shadowfire at the center, her silver flame dimmed to faint glimmers beneath her skin.

Riven landed in a blast of dual-colored light—gold and silver wings flaring wide. The ground cracked beneath the shockwave.

The Sovereign straightened on his throne, shadows swirling around him like a cloak.

"You survived," he said softly. "How disappointing. I had hoped the Golden Fire would burn you hollow."

Riven's fire sharpened into blazing armor along his limbs. "Let her go."

The Sovereign rose from the throne. "No."

He lifted a hand.

A spear of voidfire materialized and hurled toward Riven with enough force to shatter mountains.

Riven caught it.

Caught it.

For a moment, even the Sovereign froze.

Riven clenched his fist— and the spear dissolved in a burst of gold-white flame.

The Sovereign's eyes narrowed. "So the Firebound awakens at last."

Riven stepped forward, fire building under his skin. "You wanted a war."

He ignited. "You've found one."

Their first collision was silent—

—and then the world exploded.

Shadow and flame collided in a swirling vortex that razed half the throne hall.
Stone cracked.
Voidlight bled into the air.
Flame cut through shadow, shadow devoured flame.

Riven moved like a comet.
The Sovereign countered like a collapsing star.

Their blows echoed across worlds.

And Lyra watched in horror as the man she loved fought a god.

The Sovereign gestured sharply, and her chains tightened, pulling her closer as Riven battled his way toward them.

"Shall we finish our conversation?" His voice slid across her skin like ice.

Lyra gasped through the pain. "I don't want anything from you."

He tilted his head. "That is where you are wrong, child."

A tendril of shadow pressed against her chest.

Lyra screamed—but the pain wasn't physical.

It was a memory.

A memory she never knew she had.

A woman crying in the dark.
A cradle carved of obsidian.
A baby with silver hair…
and a father made of shadow.

Lyra sobbed. "No… no—that isn't real—"

The Sovereign's smile was soft and cruel. b"Your mother was a Fair Folk.

Your father was a shadow."

Lyra shook her head violently. "I'm not your daughter!"

"But you are." His voice deepened. "Your flame is not simply Vaelrion's spark…it is shadowfire. *My* fire."

Her heart twisted.

Her flame flickered black for a moment.

And that moment nearly broke her.

Riven saw her break.

That single flicker of black in her flame hit him harder than any of the Sovereign's blows.

He roared, igniting with gold-white fury and blasting back a wave of shadow that hurled even the Sovereign several steps.

Riven sprinted for Lyra, wings cutting through the darkness like twin meteors.

The Sovereign snarled: "She is mine."

"No." Riven's voice was fire, steel, and heartbreak. "She is *herself.*"

He reached Lyra—crushed the shadow-chains with a surge of dual flame and caught her as she fell.

Lyra collapsed against him, shaking. "Riven… she said… he said I'm his…"

Riven pulled her tight to his chest. "You are not."

She sobbed harder. "But he showed me—I saw it—I saw him—"

Riven's forehead touched hers. His flame wrapped around her silver fire, steadying it, warming it, pushing the blackness away.

"Your flame is yours. You choose what you are."

Her breath steadied. Her fire brightened. She whispered, "Then I choose you."

Riven's chest tightened. He kissed her forehead, fire brushing fire. "Then we burn together."

* * *

Far from the Shadow Realm, in the shattered ruins of Elderglen—Auren lay in a pool of molten gold.

His scales had cracked.
His breath came in ragged gasps.
His wings were torn.

97

The Rite of Sundering had taken its toll.

He tried to stand.

His legs buckled.

"Riven… Lyra…" His voice shook, smoke curling from his jaws. "Hurry…" He closed his eyes.

Inside his mind, he saw Vaelrion's flame—
the memory of the First Dragon—
and its voice spoke gently.

…you broke the law…
you tore the Veil…
and now you must pay the price…

Auren bowed his head. "I accept it."

…your life for theirs…

Auren shuddered——but did not hesitate. "Gladly."

His body began to dim.
His fire flickered weakly.

He whispered one last plea: "Let me live long enough to see them return…"

The wind answered.
The Veil shimmered.

And the dragon closed his eyes.

He did not die.
Not yet.

But he would.

Soon.

CHAPTER SIXTEEN:
The true battle begins — and the Shadow Realm trembles

Riven set Lyra gently behind him, his wings flaring wide and bright enough to cast shadows that had never known light.

The Sovereign stepped forward from the swirling void, robes of shadow trailing across the floor like black smoke.

His voice was low, thunder crawling beneath each word: "Firebound. Come and be broken."

Riven didn't wait.

He launched himself forward—

—and the Sovereign met him with a storm of shadows.

Flame and darkness collided in a blinding explosion that cracked the obsidian floor. Riven's fists, wrapped in molten gold-white light, hammered against the Sovereign's defenses. For every blow Riven landed, the Sovereign absorbed two.

Riven was stronger now.
But the Sovereign was endless.

Every strike of Riven's flame tore a piece of the Shadow Realm apart. Every counterblow from the Sovereign made the flames flicker dangerously in Riven's chest.

"You cannot win, boy," the Sovereign growled. "Your fire is borrowed. Mine is eternal."

Riven spat blood and golden sparks. "Then I'll burn forever."

Their next clash lit the realm like a dying star.

As the Sovereign and Riven battled, the shadows behind them stirred.

Dravaryn stepped from the darkness, his obsidian armor cracked from their earlier fight, voidfire flickering weakly.

Lyra tensed.

Riven sensed him instantly. "Stay back, Dravaryn."

But Dravaryn did not lift his blade. He looked between Riven, Lyra, and the Sovereign.

Something changed in his eyes.

A fracture.
A flicker.
A memory.

The Sovereign hissed: "My champion. Kill them."

Dravaryn stepped forward…and fell to one knee. "My Sovereign."
His blade clattered to the floor. "Forgive me."

The Sovereign's shadow coiled in warning. "What is this?"

Dravaryn raised his head slowly. "My allegiance was sworn to your flame," he said softly. "But it is not your flame that burns strongest anymore."

He looked at Riven.

At Lyra.

At the dual flame.

And bowed.

"My allegiance belongs to the Firebound."

The Sovereign roared — a sound of betrayal so ancient and raw the entire realm shuddered. "TRAITOR!"

Dravaryn's chest erupted in voidfire as the Sovereign smote him across the hall.

He slid to a stop at Lyra's feet — bleeding shadow, gasping. "Save him," he whispered. "Save the flame…"

Then darkness swallowed him.

Dravaryn was gone.

Lyra staggered backward, the revelation of Dravaryn's betrayal hitting almost as hard as the Sovereign's claim of her heritage.

The Sovereign turned his attention to her. "Little wildfire…" His voice coiled like a serpent. "Show him what you really are."

He raised his hand—

—and Lyra's silver flame exploded into black.

A scream tore from her throat as her fire spiraled uncontrollably, biting into the realm around her. Dark tendrils of shadow coiled through her light, twisting it, reshaping it.

Lyra dropped to her knees. "No—NO—I choose the light—"

But the shadowfire fought back.

The Sovereign stood over her, smiling. "You cannot deny your birthright."

Riven broke from the clash and sprinted toward her. "LYRA!"

Her eyes lifted—

—and for a heartbeat, they were black.

"Stay back," she choked. "I'll hurt you."

Riven grabbed her face gently, ignoring the flames scorching his skin. "Then burn me."

Her black flames convulsed.
Her silver flame struggled.
Her heart tore.

Riven pressed his forehead to hers. "I'm not leaving you.
You hear me?
I'm not leaving."

For a moment—

Her fire paused.

Her breath steadied.

Her silver flame glowed beneath the shadowfire like a buried star.

Lyra whispered: "Help me choose."

Riven whispered back: "Choose us."

Her flame surged.

CHAPTER SEVENTEEN:
Auren's Final Stand

Back in Elderglen, the Veil rippled, unstable from Auren's forbidden rite.

Auren—bleeding, broken, fading—felt the fire of the Firebound flare through the realms.

He lifted his head weakly. "Good…they fight…"

His vision dimmed.

His heart slowed.

He had burned too much.

His scales dulled.

His wings fell limp.

Auren whispered: "I am sorry…I cannot…stay…"

Darkness crept over his mind—

—but then something warm touched him.

A spark.

A pulse.

A whisper, ancient as creation.

…not yet, my child…

Auren gasped as warmth surged through him.

Vaelrion's Echo
the last remnant of the First Flame—
flowed into Auren's failing heart.

His eyes snapped open, glowing molten gold-white.

He rose, flames pouring off his wings.

A miracle.

A gift.

A burden.

Auren was alive.

"Hold on, Riven…Lyra…I'm coming."

He launched himself toward the Veil, wings blazing with creation's first fire.

* * *

The Shadow Realm cracked under the weight of three forces rising at once:

Riven's awakened fire.
Lyra's ascending flame.
The Sovereign's ancient shadow.

The air detonated as the final confrontation began.

The Sovereign's body shimmered, then split down the middle like a shell cracking open. Black flame poured out. His humanoid form fell away—and an ancient being rose in its place.

A towering shape built from smoke and starlight, wings stretching like eclipsed constellations. His eyes were twin abysses. A crown of broken void-fire circled his skull.

He was no longer a king.

He was a primordial.

A beast that predated flame itself.

The Shadowborn Sovereign roared.

Reality trembled.

Shadows peeled off the walls like flayed skin, swirling around their master in a storm of unraveling darkness.

"Children of fire," he thundered, "come and be unmade."

Riven stepped forward, golden-white wings blazing behind him. "Not today."

Lyra stood at his side. Her silver flame rose like a moonlit tide…

…and for the first time, her shadow fire rose with it.

Her eyes glowed — half silver, half black.
Two flames.
Two parents.
One destiny.

Auren landed behind them, molten gold dripping from his scales, still alive when he should not be.

The Sovereign laughed.

"So the last of Vaelrion's brood crawls to watch its children die."

Auren growled, fire licking his teeth. "Children? They will become what destroys you."

Lyra's breath shuddered.

Silver flame erupted across her body — bright, holy, alive.

Then the black fire followed — sinuous, dangerous, hungry.

They clashed inside her chest.

Light.
Shadow.

Truth.
Origin.

"Riven…" she whispered, terrified. "I can't control it."

He took her hands. "You don't have to. You just have to choose."

She stared at her trembling palms. "Choose what?"

"Choose who you are."

She closed her eyes.

For a moment — the silver flame won.

Then the shadowfire surged.

Her body convulsed, back arching in agony.

The Sovereign whispered from the darkness: "Come to me, daughter…"

Lyra screamed—

—and then something inside her aligned.

Lightfire and Shadowfire collided and fused into something *new*. A silver-black flame unfurled across her skin, patterns blooming like wings of starlight.

Her hair lifted in a halo of burning silver and shadow.

Her eyes glowed white.

For the first time, her voice carried two tones:

"I am not yours."
"I am not your weapon."
"I am my own fire."

Her ascension lit the Shadow Realm like a second sun.

Riven's flame roared in response to hers. They stood together.

Their wings overlapped, gold-silver and silver-black forming a radiant corona.

The Sovereign unfurled his massive shadow-wings.

Three titanic forces slammed together:

Primordial Shadow
First Fire's Echo
Ascended Moonfire

The impact shattered the throne, cracked the sky of the Shadow Realm, and sent ripples through the Veil itself.

Auren breathed: "They will tear the worlds apart..."

The Sovereign struck first — tendrils of voidfire slicing through the air like blades.

Riven deflected with a torrent of golden flame.

Lyra countered with spiraling silver-black fire that coiled around Riven's and amplified it.

Together, they pressed forward.

The Sovereign began to falter.

But the cost was rising.

Riven's chest glowed too brightly.

His flame burned too fast.

The Golden Fire was devouring him.

Auren knew it.

Lyra felt it.

Riven… hid it.

He roared, pushing the Sovereign back with a blast that shook planets.

The Sovereign reeled, cracks forming across his vast shadow-body. He whispered in disbelief: "Firebound…you would die for her."

Riven's answer was a scream of fire. "YES."

And he meant every syllable.

Because Riven had realized something:

The only way to kill the Sovereign was to burn him from the inside—
to unleash the full Golden Fire—
and that would incinerate him completely.

He took a step forward.

Lyra grabbed him. "Riven, NO!"

His eyes softened. "It's the only way."

Lyra slammed her fist against his chest. "You die, I die. Do you hear me?"

He cupped her face. "Then let me save you before either flame takes you."

Her voice broke. "I love you—"

"I know."

He turned, wings rising for the final strike.

The Sovereign roared—
the world began to collapse—
Riven's fire surged—

But Lyra stepped in front of him.

Silver-black wings flared. "No."

Riven froze. "Lyra—"

She smiled through tears. "You gave me your life once. Now I give you mine."

And she unleashed her ascended flame —

not at the Sovereign —
but into Riven.

Her silver-black fire wrapped around his gold-white flame, stabilizing it, strengthening it, transforming it.

Riven screamed — not in pain, but in power.

Lyra fell to her knees, dimming.

Auren roared in horror.

But it was too late.

Riven's wings ignited into pure cosmic flame.

His heart became a star.

His body became the conduit of two ancient powers.

He was no longer the Broken Flame.

He was no longer even the Firebound.

He became the First Flame Reborn.

He rose into the air and whispered to the Sovereign: "You took everything from me. And still—I choose the light."

Riven detonated.

Gold.
Silver.
Shadow.
Light.

A star exploded in the heart of the Shadow Realm.

And the Sovereign died screaming.

CHAPTER EIGHTEEN:
The Dawn After Shadow

Lyra gasped awake on soft moss. Warm sunlight spilled over her face. Birdsong drifted through a gentle morning breeze. The air smelled of pine and honey and distant fireflowers.

She sat up slowly, blinking.

She was back in the mortal world — in the Valley of Ash, where the dragons slept.

The last thing she remembered was giving her flame to Riven.
His face, illuminated in gold and silver.
His voice saying her name.
Then the explosion…

Her fingers trembled. "Riven?"

No answer.

Her heart lurched as she pushed herself to her feet, calling louder: "Riven!"

The valley remained quiet. Too quiet.

Lyra pressed her hand to her chest.
Her flame flickered — soft, silver-black, alive.

"Please," she whispered. "Please come back to me."

And then—

A faint warmth brushed her cheek.

Not sunlight.

A spark.

A presence she knew better than her own heartbeat.

111

She turned sharply—

—but saw only the valley.

A deep rumble shook the air behind her. The earth trembled.

Lyra spun around.

Auren staggered through the trees, wings drooping, scales cracked like cooling glass. His breaths were shallow, but his eyes — molten gold — were gentle.

"You're alive," Lyra breathed.

Auren lowered his huge head, touching his snout to her shoulder.

"Barely," he rumbled. "But enough to see the world reborn. Enough… to see you safe."

Lyra touched his warm scales, tears falling freely. "Riven… did he—?"

Auren's voice softened with sorrow and certainty. "He burned brighter than any dragon in history. The Sovereign could not withstand him."

Lyra swallowed hard. "And Riven?"

Auren's gaze lifted toward the horizon.

"His flame was scattered to the winds. But flame… always seeks a hearth."

* * *

The air shifted.

Magic hummed through the valley.

All around them, the dragon eggs embedded in the cliffs glowed faintly — as if waking from centuries of slumber.

A breeze whispered through the treetops, shimmering with silver motes. The Veil, once torn and corrupted, shimmered whole — glowing with soft purple light.

The Shadowborn dissolved like mist in sunlight, fleeing back to forgotten corners.

The Fairy Courts, far away, felt the ripple and lowered their weapons for the first time in an age.

The world exhaled.

Healed.

Alive.

A new era had begun.

And Lyra stood in the center of it…

…alone.

A gentle breeze curled around her again.

Warmer this time.
Brighter.

Lyra's breath hitched.

She turned—

—and saw him.

Riven stepped out from a fold of shimmering light, wings of molten gold and silver unfurling behind him. His hair glowed faintly, his eyes starlight-bright. His clothes were scorched but whole.

And when he smiled, the world tilted. "Took me long enough to find you."

Lyra could not breathe. Then she was running.

Running full-speed across the valley, sobbing his name, and he caught her mid-stride, sweeping her up in his arms as if he had never been gone.

She buried her face in his chest, shaking.

"I thought you died—I thought—"

Riven's voice was warm and steady. "I did."

Lyra froze.

He brushed his thumb across her cheek.

"But your fire pulled me back."

Her tears fell faster. "I gave you everything I had."

"And you gave me a reason to return." He pressed his forehead to hers.

Their flames touched—
silver-black and gold-white—
curling together like two halves of a whole.

Auren exhaled softly, sinking to the ground with relief.

The valley brightened.
New flame blossomed across the mountains.
The world moved forward.

Riven lifted Lyra's hand to his lips. "Let's build this world together, wildfire."

Lyra smiled through the tears. "Always."

And with the morning sun rising over newly awakened dragons, shadows banished, and the Veil healed…

they kissed — and the world bloomed.

* * *

The wedding took place in the Valley of Ash at sunrise.

Dragons perched along the cliffs, their wings glimmering with refracted fire; the air was filled with drifting petals of silver flame — Lyra's signature magic, dancing softly around her.

Riven stood at the center of the valley in a tunic of white and gold, his wings folded behind him like twin suns. His eyes were so full of awe he barely remembered to breathe.

Lyra walked toward him along a path lit by glowing runes. Her dress was a river of starlight — silver-black flame woven through soft silk, the colors of her two heritages in perfect harmony.

Auren lay curled nearby like a guardian mountain, his golden scales bright in the morning sun. He watched her with soft, warm pride.

When Lyra reached Riven, she took both his hands.

Riven whispered: "I've waited lifetimes for this."

Lyra smiled. "Then let's make this one last."

They exchanged vows — hers spoken in the language of flame, his in ancient fairy-tongue. Their flames rose together, spiraling upward, spiraling inward, merging in a brilliant burst above their joined hands.

Auren rumbled approvingly.

Dragons roared across the valley.

And when Riven kissed Lyra, the petals of fire danced wildly around them.

* * *

Night fell gently over the Valley of Ash.

The wedding torches had burned low.
The dragons had curled into their nests.
Auren slept like a golden mountain beneath the stars.

Riven and Lyra walked hand in hand along a quiet ridge above the valley. Their wings shimmered softly behind them — his gold-white, hers silver-black — casting rippling light on the stones.

The world was quiet.

For the first time in their lives… There was no chaos, no flight, no fear.

Lyra leaned into him. "It feels unreal," she whispered. "A whole world without running."

Riven brushed his thumb along her jaw. "Then let's learn how to stand still."

She smiled and tugged him closer until their foreheads touched. Their flames rose — not in battle, not in defense, but in the gentle way fire dances when it feels safe.

Silver sparks curled around his fingers.

Gold light warmed her skin.

"The Firebound," she murmured. "What does that make us now?"

Riven kissed her slow and soft, his breath mingling with hers. "Husband and wife."

Lyra pulled him down into the grass, laughter bubbling from her lips. He followed gladly, wings curling protectively around them as stars reflected in his eyes.

116

They lay beneath the oak that had watched the valley for centuries.

Her head on his chest. His arms around her. Nothing between them but warmth.

"Stay," Lyra whispered.

"Always," Riven answered without hesitation.

Their flames wove together — gold, silver, shadow, moonlight — forming a single quiet glow beneath the night sky.

And for the first time since the world nearly broke…they slept in peace.

CHAPTER NINTEEN:
Auren

After the ceremony, Auren curled around a nest of freshly awakened dragon eggs — the next generation born in a world without shadow.

One egg in particular glowed with warm gold.

Auren hummed deep in his chest. "You will fly sooner than I did," he murmured.

Riven leaned against his flank. "Stay with us."

Auren's eyes half-closed. "I will. For as long as the flame permits."

He drifted into restful sleep — alive, peaceful, surrounded by those he saved.

At dawn, a soft cracking sound echoed through the valley. Auren lifted his heavy head, blinking away sleep.

One of the eggs — the gold-flecked one — shook and split, revealing a tiny snout the color of sunrise. The hatchling blinked huge amber eyes and squeaked in confusion.

Lyra gasped softly.

Riven grinned.

Auren bent low, his voice rumbling like distant thunder. "Welcome, little flame."

The hatchling crawled onto his snout, tiny claws tapping against his scales. She chirped, nuzzling the warm surface.

Auren closed his eyes for a moment, overwhelmed.

"Her name," he said formally, "is Vaelira."

Lyra's breath caught.

"After Vaelrion?"

Auren nodded. "And after the world, your flames have restored."

Riven bowed his head in respect.

Vaelira flapped her small wings, scattering sparks across the valley — the first dragon born into an age of light rather than shadow.

And Auren watched her proudly, heart full, knowing he would live long enough to teach her how to fly.

EPILOGUE

And so the world breathed again.

The Veil mended.
The dragons stirred.
The Fair Folk laid down their grievances.
Shadow fled before sunrise.

And in the Valley of Ash, where legends once whispered of ruin, two flames —
gold and silver —
light and shadow —
rose together as one, promising a future forged not by prophecy, but by choice.

Riven and Lyra stood at the dawn of a new age…

…and the world, for the first time in a thousand years, burned with hope.

The Firebound were home.

PROPHECY OF THE FIREBOUND

(spoken by the last surviving Oracle of Elderglen as they are crowned)

The Oracle stepped forward — an elderly fae with silver-veined wings and a voice that carried the weight of centuries.

She lifted her staff and intoned:

"When shadow and star are born in the same breath,
and flame rises from what was once broken,
the Firebound shall stand at the dawn of a new age."

The crowd fell silent.

The Oracle continued:

"Two flames where one should be.
A heart of silver.
A heart of gold.
Together, they shall mend the Veil…
and remake its light."

She turned to Riven:

"The Broken Flame restored."

Then to Lyra:

"The Daughter of Shadow and Moon."

And as they clasped hands:

"As long as these flames choose one another,
darkness shall never return unchecked.
This is the age of fire renewed."

Auren bent his massive head and let them place the twin coronets upon it so he could press his forehead against theirs.

"May your flames burn gently," he murmured.

THE BARD'S FINAL SONG — "THE FIREBOUND PROMISE"

Later that night, during the celebration, a traveling bard stood atop a boulder and plucked a soft melody on a pearwood lute.

His voice carried through the valley:

"THE FIREBOUND PROMISE"

When gold met silver in shadow's keep,
And fire answered fire's deep call,
A broken flame learned how to burn,
A world once lost began to fall.

But from the ash new dawns arise,
Two hearts entwined in fiercest light;
The Firebound rose hand in hand,
To drive the darkness from the night.

A dragon's roar, a lover's vow,
A sovereign cast to starless sea;
The world remade by flame and hope,
By those who dared: 'Let us be free.'

So sing the names of Riven bold,
And Lyra, silver-heart of flame;
The fire they forged shall never die—
For all the world now bears their name.

www.ingramcontent.com/pod-product-compliance
Lightning Source LLC
Chambersburg PA
CBHW061252170626
46809CB00007B/2963